A Long and Lonely Ride

A Long and Lonely Ride

Helen Fogwill Porter

Breakwater
100 Water Street
P.O. Box 2188
St. John's, Newfoundland, Canada
A1C 6E6

The Publisher gratefully acknowledges the financial support of The Canada Council, which has helped make this publication possible.

The Publisher acknowledges the financial support of the Cultural Affairs Division of the Department of Municipal and Provincial Affairs, Government of Newfoundland and Labrador, which has made this publication possible.

The author acknowledges The Canada Council, the Newfoundland Writers' Guild, W.H. New, Kent Thompson, Marilyn Best, Alice Munro, Edna Alford, Fred Cogswell, the Newfoundland Provincial Reference Library, Bill Fogwill and the late Susanna Porter.

Cover art by Rae Perlin, entitled In The Luxembourg Gardens, *used by kind permission of Kathy Porter.*

Some of the stories in this collection have already appeared in *Fireweed, A Way with Words, The Newfoundland Quarterly, Twelve Newfoundland Short Stories, The Livyere, Voices Down East, Stories from Atlantic Canada, The Atlantic Anthology, The Antigonish Review, Baffles of Wind and Tide* and *Pottersfield Portfolio*.

Canadian Cataloguing in Publication Data

Porter, Helen, 1930-
   A long and lonely ride
   ISBN 1-55081-011-1

I . Title.
PS8581.077L66   1991   C813'.54   C91-097551-5
PR9199.3.P67L66   1991

© 1991 Helen Fogwill Porter
ALL RIGHTS RESERVED. No part of this work covered by the copyright hereon may be reproduced or used in any form or by any means—graphic, electronic or mechanical—without the prior written permission of the publisher. Any request for photocopying, recording, taping or information storage and retrieval systems of any part of this book shall be directed in writing to the Canadian Reprography Collective, 379 Adelaide Street West, Suite M1, Toronto, Ontario M5V 1S5. This applies to classroom usage as well.

*For my children
Kathy, Anne, Johnny and Stephen*

women and men in the crowd meet and mingle,
Yet with itself every soul standeth single.

> Alice Cary 1820-1871
> American poet

Contents

In Broad Daylight	*11*
Unravelling	*22*
O Take Me As I Am	*28*
The Summer Visitors	*41*
Eva	*47*
Wintergreen *	*58*
The Plan	*63*
Walking	*77*
A Long and Lonely Ride	*79*
Moving Day	*90*
A Different Person	*95*
Mainly Because of the Meat	*105*
One Saturday	*115*

*Originally titled "The Smell of Wintergreen"

In Broad Daylight

I thought I saw Shirley Butler the other day. I was hurrying along Water Street when I passed a heavy, middle-aged woman in a black coat and slacks. She was standing by Bowring's window, looking in. There was something familiar about her; when, after I passed, I glanced back, I could see she was looking at me. It was Shirley, I'm almost sure. Her hair is not as black as it used to be. There's more grey in it than there is in mine. It's still curly though, but not at all fashionable. It wasn't fashionable all those years ago, either, not the way she wore it, but I envied anyone who had naturally curly hair.

She turned back toward the window and stared in again. I wondered if I should go and speak to her. I'm always meeting people that I used to know and wondering if I should speak to them or not. They're probably wondering the same thing about me.

Even if Shirley did recognize me I'm sure she wouldn't expect me to recognize her. It was only that one day, really. We probably wouldn't have met at all if Chuck and Bob hadn't been friends. Even though I hadn't met her before she looked familiar to me. I probably used to see her on my way to and from school.

Shirley wasn't around the day I met Chuck. Or at least as far as I know she wasn't. There were a lot of people in the park that day, though. We had a holiday from school in celebration of the King's birthday, which was really at quite a different time of the year but, for some reason, always celebrated in June. The weather was gorgeous, sunny and clear and warm, but not too hot. It was unusual for us to get such good weather in June.

It was our first time in the park for the year, and there was always something special about that. The swimming pool didn't open until the first of July, no matter how hot the weather was, so we just walked from the Bungalow to the Rosary Garden to the playground. At fifteen we were too old for the playground, of course, but we still liked to fool around on the swings and the monkey climber, just so we could shout at each other about how childish we were. I had on my white shorts, and I kept looking down at my legs. They were kind of pale, the way legs always are the first time they're displayed bare after the winter. Maybe I should have worn leg-paint. But I probably would have got it all patchy, and that would have looked worse. Secretly, I was vain of my legs. They were long and well-shaped. They're still long, but the thighs are lumpy now, and there are ugly purple vein marks all over the place. I had hardly any breasts to speak of, and I've never been pretty, so I supposed it was only fair that I should have something worth looking at.

Ruth and Audrey were with me. Ruth, who is my cousin and therefore someone I've known all my life, had changed overnight from a sturdy, rosy-cheeked child with stringy dark hair into a startlingly attractive girl with a shining page-boy and a thirty-six inch bust. She was short, and all the rest of her was small. This made her breast size really dramatic. She was aware of it, too, and wore an uplift brassiere that pushed the lovely cleavage to the top of her round-necked peasant blouse. Some of the boys called her "Coke bottle legs" but that was probably only because there was nothing else wrong with her. I envied her more than I've ever envied anyone else in my life.

Audrey's bust was big, too, but she was heavy all over and this tended to cancel out the effect. She had, however, already had one steady boyfriend with whom she used to lie on the kitchen day-bed nights when her parents were out and she was minding her two little brothers. I envied her, too, but I didn't want to be fat. And I hadn't liked her boyfriend very much. He was only about a year older than herself, and not much to look at. I never really knew what she saw in him.

"Lots of soldiers around today," said Ruth as we walked back toward the Bungalow from the playground. We had just about enough money for a Coke each besides our bus-fare home. Or our truck-fare. At that time, open trucks with benches along the sides and a rope across the back were still being used for passengers. Of course if we spent all our money we could always hitchhike home, or thumb a ride, as we called it. But this was strictly forbidden, and we tried not to disobey our parents any more than was absolutely necessary. We told each other it was all right to accept rides from women drivers, or in cars that had a woman in the front seat with the driver. But most of the time we rode in the truck.

The Bungalow verandah was crowded. In order to get to the counter we had to pass a table where three young soldiers were sitting. We took special pains not to look at them. They were Americans, we knew that by their well-fitting uniforms. The Canadian soldiers always looked as if their uniforms had been made for someone else.

"Oh, boy, look at Jane Russell!" we heard one of them say. Audrey and I hoped he was talking about Ruth. Even though we were jealous of her, we were proud of her figure. It was the next best thing to looking that way ourselves.

The three of them were still there when we came back with our drinks. We stood still for a moment, looking for a place to sit down.

"Hey, Blondie," said one of the soldiers, a stocky fellow with a reddish-brown crew cut. "Hey, Blondie, there's three seats here."

We didn't turn around, but we didn't move on, either. Blondie. He must have been talking about me. My hair was light brown, but I liked to describe it as ash-blonde. My sister Alice called me a dirty blonde but I didn't like the sound of that. Ruth and Audrey were both dark, so he couldn't have meant them. Blondie. It was the first time anyone had ever called me that.

"Come on, girls, we don't bite," said one of the others. We turned around then, after nudging each other. What harm could it do to sit with them? It was the middle of the afternoon. Our parents never worried about us doing anything wrong in broad daylight.

We sat down, careful not to spill our drinks. The soldiers had finished theirs, and were smoking cigarettes. One of them, the tall, light-haired one who had made the Jane Russell remark, passed around the package. Lucky Strikes. Most of the boys we knew could only afford Royal Blends, and even then they bought them loose, a few at a time.

None of us accepted a cigarette. We smoked a little, in secret, but we hadn't mastered the casual way of holding a cigarette that we admired in older girls, and we didn't want the soldiers to know what novices we were.

They weren't very old themselves, nineteen, we found out later. Chuck, the quiet, dark-haired fellow who hadn't called out at all, was almost twenty. He looked a little like Robert Walker, whose autographed photograph I'd just sent away to *Photoplay* for.

Most of our conversation was made up of wisecracks, but the boys did manage to tell us where they were from and how long they'd been in Newfoundland. None of them had seen any action yet (they laughed when they said that) but they were anxious to. Or so they said.

Although Bob, the red-haired fellow, had been the one who called out Blondie, it was Audrey he talked to. He had probably been disappointed when he got a good look at my front. Gary, the fair-haired soldier who was the handsomest of the three, was giving all his attention to Ruth. They made a game of snatching, or trying to snatch, paper cups from each other. He only touched her hands but you could see his mind was on another part of her.

Chuck told me he came from Nebraska. I had read a novel set in Nebraska. It was called *A Lantern in Her Hand*; I cried so much over it that Mom had threatened not to let me go to the library any more. I told Chuck about the book, but he had never heard of it. He didn't read much, he said.

They insisted on buying us ice cream cones and then the six of us walked around the park together. I prayed that I wouldn't meet anyone I knew, or at least anyone who was likely to tell Mom. At that time of her life her greatest fear for her two daughters was of pregnancy before marriage. Alice was engaged to a boy she'd gone to school with who was in the Royal Navy. Mom was almost ready to breathe easily about her, although she wouldn't be completely relaxed until the wedding day.

"I know you're too sensible a girl to get involved with any of those servicemen," she said to me from time to time. "Of course you're only fifteen but the stories I've heard...." She always left the sentence unfinished. One night I overheard her telling my father that she thanked God I looked so young. Still, she never let me leave the house without a warning.

"Look after yourself, now," she'd say. She was never very specific. Or, "Don't be too late coming home." Or, worst of all, "I'm so thankful to have daughters I can trust."

On the way home in the truck Gary's arm was right around Ruth's shoulder, and Bob was playing with Audrey's hand. Some of the other girls aboard were necking quite shamelessly with soldiers they had met that day. Chuck sat very close to me, but he didn't try to touch me.

"When are you going to the park again?" he asked me as we were driving out Waterford Bridge Road. I had told him I'd soon be getting off.

My heart was beating so fast I could hardly find breath to reply. "Sunday," I said, swallowing hard. " I'll probably be going in Sunday afternoon." I hardly ever went to the park on Sundays except occasionally in July and August when Sunday School was closed for the summer. Ever since I'd stopped going to Sunday School myself I'd been teaching a class of six-year-old boys. But "Sunday," I repeated, half to myself. (I'd heard Chuck tell Bob he was off Sunday.) Then it was time for me to get off the truck.

"Good-bye," said Chuck. "See you." All the way up the sweet-smelling tree-shaded lane that led to my street, past the greenhouses of the florist who lived there. I kept asking myself if he'd said "See you Sunday" or just "See you." Audrey and Ruth were still in the truck. They lived further downtown.

On Sunday I started early, preparing the ground. "I don't think I'll go to Sunday School today," I said before I left for church in the morning. I didn't always go to church Sunday mornings but I thought I'd better go that day to give myself some extra points.

"Why not?" Mom wasn't listening very hard. She had got up later than she'd intended and had a big dinner to cook.

"I hardly ever miss a Sunday. And there's not much going on right now. They're just practising for the closing program and I've got nothing to do with that."

"Where are you going, then?" She opened the oven door to poke at the roast.

"Audrey and Ruth want me to go to the park with them." I tried to sound as though I only wanted to do my friends a favour. In fact, I had spent hours trying to persuade them to come with me. Bob and Gary had not asked them when they'd be going to the park again.

All week I'd been wondering what I should wear. I knew I'd never get out of the house on a Sunday wearing shorts. I could wear a skirt with my shorts on underneath, and then take the skirt off later, but I was convinced Mom would find out somehow, and I felt I was pushing my luck enough already. I put on my red and white cotton peasant skirt, which was short and full. The new organdy blouse my grandmother had sent me for my birthday was frilly and loose, except under the arms where it scratched my skin raw. It looked nice, though.

The three of them were there again, Chuck, Gary and Bob, sitting at the same table on the Bungalow verandah. The park was even more crowded than it had been the first day. You could hardly walk anywhere without tripping over couples curled up together on the grass. The six of us walked up the river where the vegetation was wilder, less controlled than it was in the more formal part of the park. The other four dropped out of sight behind Chuck and me but we just kept on walking. He was singing softly to himself:

> You belong to my heart
> Now and forever,
> And our love had its start
> Not long ago.

It was on the Hit Parade all that summer.

Chuck asked me to meet him again the following Thursday. It wasn't a holiday but I planned to go to the park right after school. Perhaps I'd even skip school, something I'd never done in my life. This time I didn't even tell Ruth and Audrey that I was going to meet Chuck.

Thursday was chilly, with a stiff breeze. There weren't any trucks going to the park on weekdays so I thumbed my way in. I couldn't believe it was me, acting so bold. A green Pontiac stopped for me. It was driven by a thin, tired-looking woman who told me she was a nurse at the hospital near the park.

That day, without talking much, Chuck and I went straight from the Bungalow to the grassy bank that sloped steeply down to the railway track. When I was younger, I used to run there with all the other children whenever the train whistle blew, but now the park was almost deserted. Most people were working, or in school, and the weather wasn't warm enough to attract mothers with small children. Still without saying much to each other, Chuck and I sat, and later lay, on the grass. He held out his arms and I moved into them. We didn't talk about what we were doing. We must have looked like all the other couples that Ruth and Audrey and I used to trip over. We kissed a few times, but mostly we just lay there.

After that afternoon, everything else in my life became a dream. The only thing that mattered was meeting Chuck, which I did every time he asked me to. We usually went to the park, back to the grassy bank above the train track. I was surprised, and relieved, that he didn't try to do anything but hug and kiss me. I had been so sternly warned about soldiers that I hadn't really expected him to stop there. I don't know what I would have done if he hadn't. One day he put his hand on my left breast, outside the white cotton gym blouse I was wearing. He left it there for a few minutes and then he said, "Do you mind my hand where I've got it?" I didn't know what to say. I knew I shouldn't have let him touch me like that but I didn't want him to take his hand away. So I finally said, "I don't even know where it is." He left it there for the rest of the afternoon. I could feel the slight, warm pressure for days afterwards.

One afternoon, when we had been lying on the bank for about an hour, he sat up suddenly and lit a cigarette. When I sat up too I could see that he was frowning.

"What's the matter?" I asked. I had never seen him frown like that before.

"Nothing," he said. He just kept smoking and looking at the train tracks.

"There *is* something." I wanted us to be still lying there.

He looked at me, and smiled a little. "Sometimes," he said, "Sometimes I wish you were a little older."

The rest of the day was spoiled. We stayed there for a while longer, but it wasn't the same. On the way home in the truck we hardly looked at each other.

As far as I knew, we had never been seen by anyone who was likely to tell Mom. One day some boys from my school hooted up at us, but they weren't the kind who'd tell anyone's mother anything. I went hot with guilt every time Mom looked at me, and especially when she asked me where I'd been.

"Oh, just out for a walk with Ruth and Audrey," I'd say. Or, "I was downtown for a while." Or even, "I went to the park with a couple of girls from school." I was confident that Audrey and Ruth would never let Mom know the difference. Although we fell out at times we protected each other always against older people.

Ruth and Audrey weren't seeing Gary and Bob anymore. Ruth, who never stayed interested in one boy for long, had been asked out one Friday night by Clark Marshall, one of the boys from school. He was allowed to use his father's big blue Plymouth on weekends. Audrey was still interested in Bob but he seemed to have other things on his mind.

"You're the lucky one, Linda," she said to me more than once. Then, sounding surprised, "Bob told me Chuck really likes you. He must enjoy robbing the cradle."

That made me mad. Audrey and I were the same age, even if she did look older because of all that weight. But I agreed with her on one thing. I couldn't imagine what Chuck saw in me. He told me one day that my legs were just as good as Betty Grable's, and that I was nice to talk to. Since I could hardly ever think of anything to say to him I didn't really know what he meant by the last remark. But the other one, the one about my legs, I kept hearing that again and again in my head, as if I were listening to a gramophone record. I'd thought they were pretty good myself, but Betty Grable? I wasn't used to hearing comparisons like that. "It must be nice to have a brain," and "I wish I could write compositions like yours" were the kind of things boys usually said to me. Or sometimes they used me to get to know Ruth. My father, who was quiet and hard-working and a great reader, used to say sometimes: "Never mind, Linda, there's something about your face that's better than all their showy looks. You've got intelligence, and character. Anyone can see there's something *to* you." I tried to smile when he said things like that, but they didn't cheer me up at all.

One day when I met Chuck in the park Bob was there too. That was the day he had Shirley Butler with him. Her breasts were as big as Ruth's but the rest of her figure was nothing to rave over. She had curly black hair and narrow dark eyes that looked kind of sly. She was wearing brown and white checked slacks and a tight yellow blouse. She couldn't have been any more than sixteen, but she looked older.

"I think I've seen you around before," she said when Bob introduced us. He didn't ask about Audrey. It was as if he had never known her. "What school do you go to?"

"Prince of Wales," I said half-apologetically.

"Oh, that snobby place." She was nice enough, though. We all had a Coke together and she told me she was leaving school soon, and going to work in one of the big clothing factories. "I don't like learning," she said. "What's the good of it to a girl, anyway?" She looked sideways at Bob when she said that, and he whispered something in her ear that made her laugh out loud. He had never talked like that to Audrey.

When we finished our Cokes we went down to the Rosary Garden. We figured there'd be too many people on the bank near the train track, and besides it really wasn't very comfortable there. The grassy part of the Rosary Garden was flat; there was shade from the big trees.

It was a very hot day, humid and sticky, and after we had been there for a while, lying in our usual position, I began to feel uncomfortable. Perhaps it was partly because Shirley and Bob were lying not far away from us and we could hear them whispering and giggling. Except for the first couple of times when Audrey and Ruth and Gary and Bob were with us, when we spent most of our time walking around anyhow. Chuck and I had always been alone before.

I sat up and said, "Chuck, let's go and get some ice cream. My throat is parched."

Chuck seemed to be almost asleep. "I'm too lazy to move," he said into the grass. "Can't you wait a little while?"

By this time, Bob and Shirley were sitting up too. "I'd like some ice cream myself, " Bob said, stretching his arms over his head. "Tell you what, Linda, why don't you and me go get some and bring it back to these lazybones here?"

I didn't really want to go to the Bungalow with Bob but I didn't know how to get out of it. We walked away; as soon as we were out of the Rosary Garden, Bob tried to grab my hand. I snatched it away.

I wanted to run back to Chuck but I was just stubborn enough to walk on toward the Bungalow. After a few moments Bob's manner changed. He started to talk about the school he had gone to, P.S. something or other, back in Pittsburgh.

The ice cream was already half-melted by the time we got back to the Rosary Garden, but Chuck and Shirley didn't look as though they wanted any. They were lying in the exact same spot that I had left a few minutes before. Chuck's arms were around her, just as they'd been around me. The two of them looked a little embarrassed when they sat up, but they tried to talk as if nothing was any different. Without a word we handed them their ice cream cones.

"Let's go for a walk," Chuck said, holding out his free hand to me. I wouldn't take it. We walked along the path, together but not touching each other. Bob sat down beside Shirley and she calmly began to eat her dripping ice cream cone.

"What's wrong?" Chuck asked after a few minutes. "Gee, that ice cream's soft." Just as if nothing had happened.

"How could you?" I said, not looking at him.

"Oh, that." He laughed, not sounding like Chuck at all. "That didn't mean a thing."

"What about if you'd found Bob and me like that?"

"That's different," he said, and tried to take my hand again.

After that day, everything changed. I went to a movie with Chuck the next Saturday afternoon. (We never went out together at night; I had no idea what he did then.) He fell asleep in the middle of the picture and slept right through to the end. The movie was *Since You Went Away*; under other circumstances I would have loved it. I was so mad I left the theatre while Chuck was still asleep in the gallery. "That's a sin," said one of the girls from school who had seen us together. "He'll probably be locked in." I pretended I hadn't heard her. Chuck had smelled of beer that day, the first time I'd ever noticed that smell on him.

We made up after that, but it wasn't the same. We went to the park a few more times but when we lay down together I could see Shirley's face in my mind. I had never actually seen her since I got off the truck that day. I don't think she ever went out with Bob again.

A couple of weeks later Ruth and I left on the train to spend a holiday around the bay with our grandmother. We did that every summer. There were a lot of soldiers on the train but we didn't talk to any of them. The weather was beautiful and we spent most of our time standing outside on the brakes, singing, "There's a new moon over my shoulder/And an old love still in my heart."

"Whatever happened to you and Chuck?" Ruth asked. I hadn't told her anything about Shirley.

"Oh, I don't know," I said, looking back toward the town we had just left. "I suppose he was a bit too old for me."

I wrote Chuck one letter from Birchy Harbour, a casual, carefully-friendly letter, but he didn't answer. I never saw him again.

By the time we got back to town after our holiday the weather was already turning cooler. Audrey, Ruth and I went to the park once or twice but saw no familiar faces on the Bungalow verandah.

"I'm glad you don't go out so much anymore," Mom said to me one Saturday afternoon when I was sitting in the dining-room, reading. "I was saying to Mrs. Noseworthy the other day, 'It's wonderful not to have to worry about your daughters.' Poor Mrs. Armstrong, down to the church, her daughter is in the family way, you know. Some soldier." Mom was busy getting ready for Alice's wedding, which was to take place in November when Harry came home on leave.

Sometimes, when I walked down Water Street, I'd see the familiar uniform and be almost afraid to look up. But when I did, it was never the right face. After a while I hardly even expected it to be Chuck. I didn't even cry much at night any more.

I haven't thought about Chuck for years but the other day, the day I saw Shirley, it all came rushing back. She's put on weight, the same as I have, and she looked awfully tired. I probably should have spoken to her.

Unravelling

If he hadn't been so tired, David would never have gone into the Park Inn. He always avoided such places, preferring to sip his drinks with Marilyn at home or in a restaurant, or at a hotel bar with some of his colleagues. But this had been a particularly hard day and he just wasn't functioning properly. He needed a beer, or maybe two, and the Park Inn was handy. He went in and sat down at a table in the corner, adjusting his eyes to the sudden darkness.

It was restful, though, after the hard fluorescent brightness of the office. He closed his eyes for a moment, and when he opened them it did not seem quite so dark as before. He could make out shapes now, the other tables and chairs, the bartender wiping glasses, bodies slumped across tables, men sitting straight and drinking quietly, other men talking, arguing, shouting. No women. The Park Inn belonged to the old days when taverns were for men only. It wanted no truck with the new lounge idea, and as far as he knew no woman had ever crossed its doorstep, except perhaps a wife looking for her husband.

He'd better go over to the bar. No such luxury as being waited on at the tables here. As he weaved his way in and out among the other drinkers it seemed to him that he had been in the Park Inn at least once before. Or a place very much like it. He was very young at the time, certainly no more than seven, and his father had brought him in one Wednesday half-holiday. There had been some kind of round cheese biscuits in the middle of the table, wasn't there a rule then about no drinking without eating? And his father had given him sips of beer from his glass, while David screwed up his face at the unexpected bitter taste. And then he had crammed the cheese biscuits into his mouth, and his father had laughed, and called him a little glutton.

The bartender, a tired-looking man who cleared his throat constantly, deliberately finished polishing a glass before he looked at David. "What'll it be, boss?" he asked then, pretending to flick at the counter top with the cloth in his hand.

"Do you have McEwan's?" He had not really known what he was going to ask for until the words dropped out of his mouth.

"McEwan's?" The man's heavy eyebrows arched. "No, we haven't, not right now. Don't get asked for it very often. What about a Dominion, or a India?"

"India'll be fine." He didn't like India at all but then, for that matter, he didn't like McEwan's either. After paying for the beer he carried it back to the table. He opened his newspaper but it was too dark to read. People didn't read newspapers at the Park Inn. Some talked, either to themselves or their companions, some just drank, and others sat and said nothing.

He closed his eyes again, and leaned back in the chair. As a small child he used to close his eyes when he was in a hurry for something to happen. For no reason that he could identify he began to think about his sixth birthday.

"What time is it now, Mom?" he asked for the twelfth time that evening.

"Five minutes later than the last time you asked." She smiled at him from the chair near the window where she sat knitting. She was always knitting. Sometimes, when she finished a garment and had no more wool on hand, she would unravel it right back to the beginning and start all over again. He had told Marilyn that once but Marilyn didn't believe him. "You must have dreamt it," she said, but he knew it was true. And on that particular night the wool had been a lovely soft blue shade. He thought he had worn it later as a school sweater. Light blue and dark blue, the school colours were. Were there any school colours now?

"Where we going tomorrow, Mom?" He knew, of course, but he wanted to hear her say it again. She was aware of this but, as usual, she played along.

"Well, we'll get up early," she began.

"Seven o'clock," he said, unable to wait. "And we'll have pancakes for breakfast, with brown sugar sauce for you and Dad and 'lasses for me."

"And then we'll go and call for Billy," she continued.

"What about the presents?"

"Oh, surely goodness you don't want your presents in the morning. Aren't you going to wait till tea-time, like they do in the books? Perhaps there'll be something on Aunt Kate's program for you."

"In the morning," he said firmly. "I'll have Nanny's when she comes to tea, and if Aunt Kate 'nounces one I'll find that then too."

David opened his eyes and blinked a couple of times, and then he had to blink again, for he saw a man, a short, thin, erect man in a grey sports jacket, with carefully combed, thinning hair, make his way slowly between the tables, his eyes looking straight ahead. David half rose to his feet, so sure was he that he had been seen, but then, as the man continued unswervingly toward a table in the opposite corner, he sat back again. The newcomer seated himself carefully, the back of his head toward David.

"How's she goin', Mr. Dunbar?" Mr. Dunbar. That was typical, wasn't it? No first names, even here.

"Hello, Charlie" The voice was low, but clear."How about a Blue Star?"

"Comin' up, Mr. Dunbar."

David studied the back of the man's head. Funny how much brighter it seemed in here now. Eyes growing accustomed to the darkness and all that. He looked at his beer, still foamy at the top. It was lighter than McEwan's, both in colour and texture. His mother's voice, not so controlled as usual, coming from the bedroom door next to his.

"That dark ale, Doug, why do you drink it? It turns you into a savage."

He could not hear what his father was saying, but he was talking all right. He talked and talked, all night it seemed to David. The last sound he heard before slipping into sleep was his father's voice, not his words, just his voice, but the next morning his father wouldn't talk at all. His mother talked a lot then, her voice high and nervous as she got David ready for the birthday celebration. They had the pancakes, but they didn't taste very good, and at the last minute his father decided to stay home instead of going with them to pick up Billy. His mother had talked all day. All the while they were on the bus and in the park. She was still talking when they came back to the house in the late afternoon,

Nanny's parcel in her hand. Nanny had not felt like coming to tea after all, and they completely forgot to listen to Aunt Kate's program.

He looked across the room again now. The old man sitting alone at the table was signalling for another glass of beer. David looked at his own glass. Still three-quarters full. As he raised it to his lips the smell of the place almost overpowered him. Funny, how much stronger the smell was at the Park Inn than at the new lounges and clubs.

His mother, opening all the windows, shaking powder under the cushions, flicking drops of Evening in Paris cologne all over the room. No spray deodorants then. But the heaviness remained. Sometimes she put a thick coat of paste wax on the hall canvas, and the smells got all intermingled and David began to feel sick.

He took another gulp of beer and looked again at the man in the grey jacket. He was deep into his second glass now, living for it, loving it. David's own glass was half-full, and already he wanted to go to the bathroom. He took another swallow.

His mother, knitting again, something long and yellow this time. "But, Doug, I needed that money," she was saying, her eyes never leaving the needles. "I told you I needed that money."

Again his father's voice was indistinct. The words were thick, like the air in the room, but the sound continued until his mother put down her knitting and said, "I'm going to bed, Doug." And then, as she climbed the stairs, his father was right behind her, stumbling a little but managing to keep up with her, talking, talking, all the time.

"You'd prevoke our Saviour." Her voice was tired.

"**Pro**-voke, my dear, not **pre**-voke." His voice was clear, just for a moment, and then David could no longer hear what he was saying, but again the voice went on and on into the night.

David was just about to look for the toilet when the man in the grey jacket got to his feet and made his way unhesitatingly to the door marked Gents. Why Gents when there was no Ladies? He watched the man walk straight, straight as a birch rod, across the floor.

"Your father's a very smart man, David." His mother wasn't just trying to convince him, or herself. She really believed it, and it was true, of course. But she was smart, too. She was quick at sums, and a real whiz at spelling. She was good at telling stories too, though perhaps not quite as good as his father, who acted out all the parts.

"I went down with a long-tailed rat and a bucket full of fat...." What came next? David had never seen that particular piece of verse in any of the children's books he had come across since. What an odd thing it was to tell to children, anyhow, but he had loved it. Especially the way his father told it.

"I wouldn't stay with him, Enid. I've told you that before, and I'm telling you again. You've only got the one child, why don't you get out while you're still young?" His grandmother had said those words, or variations of them, so many times. And his mother's reply was always the same.

"He's as good as gold when he's not drinking, Mom. And you know he's never laid a hand on me." The knitting was navy blue this time, a pair of socks for her brother Herb in the Royal Navy.

"And he better not, either, not while I'm on this earth." His grandmother's face always turned crimson when she talked that way. "But there's other things besides hitting. If your father had ever talked to me the way...."

His mother's lips tightened; she went to the stove to steep the tea.

The first time David heard those crude and cruel words snarled out by his father—perhaps it hadn't really been the first time he heard them, but the first time he understood them—he had thought it was some sort of game. They were the kind of words Bottles Morgan used, and Harry O'Brien. Surely it couldn't be his father—that quiet, reserved, almost solemn man—calling his mother such filthy names. But it was his voice, and as David grew older he heard the words more and more often, until he learned to shut them out.

The old man was coming back from the toilet now. Was he really an old man? From that distance he didn't look like one—the lean, spare body, the erect carriage, were almost the same as they had always been. He went to the bar, and stood politely while Charlie served another customer.

"When are you going to get some McEwan's in, Charlie?" he asked.

"No call for it, Mr. Dunbar," Charlie said, clearing his throat before he spoke.

The man leaned forward on the bar. "How about a whiskey, then?" he asked, so softly David could barely hear him.

The bartender seemed uneasy. "Are you sure, Mr. Dunbar? Remember what happened the last time."

The old man—he did look like an old man now—dropped his arms to his sides, tipped back his head and said, "Are you suggesting to me what I should or shouldn't drink, Charles?" There was a slight trace of a drawl, and just the faintest twinge of an exaggerated upper-class accent.

The bartender sighed, shrugged his shoulders and moved back toward the bottles behind the bar. The old man half-turned, one elbow on the counter, and waited without speaking.

David raised his glass to his lips and then put it down again. He didn't want any more of that stuff. When the old man, glass held carefully in both hands, had seated himself again at his table, David stood up and made his way quickly to the door. He wanted another drink, perhaps several more drinks, but not at the Park Inn. As David stepped into the street the old man lifted his glass and took a long, sweet swallow.

O Take Me As I Am

Whenever things got too much for her, Noreen went to church.

"I think I'll go to church tonight," she told the family one Sunday in October.

"What's wrong, now, Mom?" Dinah asked. "The world too much with you?"

"No." Noreen's voice was sharp. She couldn't help speaking sharply when someone read her thoughts. People were always doing that in this family. "I just feel like going to church, that's all."

"Do you want the car?" Richard asked, looking up from his book. She had thought he hadn't even heard her.

"No, thanks, I'd rather walk. It's a beautiful night out."

Later, as she walked up the quiet street, very slowly because she didn't want to be too early, she thought about the word *church*. Years ago, when she first started going to the Salvation Army, nobody ever called it *church*, particulary the Salvationists themselves. They went to *meeting*, or *prayers*, or, a little later on, to *service*. Andrew Martin had always called it *zervice*. It wasn't an affectation, just a natural variation, the way some people said *f* for *v* and *azipper* for *zipper*. In the outports people often used the word *barracks*, which gradually gave way to *citadel*, if they were just talking about the building. Never, never *church*. But now everyone said *church*, even the faithful ones who, unlike herself, went every week, often twice on Sunday.

Her children didn't go to church at all. They had each stopped in the early teens. Not many of their friends went either. It seemed strange to her for young people not to go to church. She was fairly certain it must be her fault that hers didn't go. Most things were. Richard had stopped going too, but she didn't blame herself for that. After all, she hadn't brought him up.

As far as church was concerned, she could divide her life into phases. When she was a child she always went to church and Sunday School at the same United Church that she'd been christened in, and where her father and mother had been married. As she remembered it, she had never even considered not going. She was in the Mission Band, too, and had recited a poem that began, "Jesus loves every child/Black, brown and white" in the concert that was held in the Lecture Hall to raise money for the children in Trinidad. Her mother had coached her. She had also won a prize for bringing the most money in her Easter envelope. The money, of course, had to be earned. Noreen had washed two very dirty flags for her grandfather and he had paid her five dollars for the job. The other children envied her. They'd have had to wash dishes for weeks to earn that much.

Under a street light, she looked at her watch. It got dark so early now. Still only a quarter to seven. Well, she couldn't dawdle anymore. Perhaps there'd be a singspiration before the service started. Horrible word, but she enjoyed singing, even though she couldn't carry a tune. Church was about the only place she could sing and not be noticed.

Sure enough, there was a singsong going on. At the front of the citadel, on the rostrum above the mercy seat, a young man stood. He had a piano accordion slung around his neck and he swayed from side to side as he sang. Beside him a teenage boy played softly on a guitar. The citadel was about three-quarters full. Some people sat with their heads bowed, others were bolt upright, and a few knelt at the front. Noreen went in quietly and found a seat near the back. It seemed to be more of a prayer meeting than a singspiration. The words were familiar:

> I have a Saviour, He's pleading in Glory,
> A dear loving Saviour, though earth friends be few;
> And now He is watching in tenderness o'er me,
> And O that my Saviour were your Saviour too!

And then the chorus:

> *For you I am praying, for you I am praying,*
> *For you I am pray-ay-ing, I'm praying for you.*

Noreen felt the hot tears behind her eyes. Oh, my God, not already. She always forgot that church did this to her, especially certain songs and certain churches. People who noticed, if anyone did, might take it as a sign of religious conviction, but she knew better. Or thought she did. Surely it was just an association of ideas, memories of other meetings, other services. Other people.

Other people. She thought of old Major Hammond, his thick white hair tousled, his red guernsey showing through the open tunic. He used to play the concertina. It was years since she had heard a concertina. The Major had tried to teach some of the bandsmen to play it. Andrew had been very good at it, but then he seemed to be good at almost everything he took up.

The officer at Birchy Harbour had played one too. It helped with the singing; there was no piano. Noreen thought of Ruby Graves, her long dark brown hair plaited and wound neatly around her head, the saintly expression on her face as she knelt at her chair on the platform of the barracks at Birchy Harbour. She thought also of the whispers about Ruby, and what she herself had seen on the Pond Bridge that Sunday afternoon. She thought of Uncle Eleazer, of Walter, of her mother and her grandfather, of her own children who, when they were small, had actually cried to go to Sunday School.

She reached into her purse for her glasses. The tears weren't so noticeable when she was wearing glasses. Just as she was about to take them out of their case she remembered that girl out on the west coast, the one Laura had told her about. The girl who, when she finally allowed herself to believe that she was pregnant with no hope of getting married, had sat in a rocking-chair all day long and picked her Salvation Army bonnet to pieces. Noreen put the glasses back in her purse. She wouldn't be needing them after all, not right now, anyway.

She realized that she'd been involved with the Army much longer than with what her mother still persisted in calling "your own church." She had started going to the meetings when she was fifteen. As long as she was categorizing, she might as well call that her second church phase. Sometimes she thought it was the most important one, but perhaps that was only because what happens in the teens always seems more important, both at the time and later, than anything else.

When people joked about Jimmy Carter's religion, she wondered whether those same people would laugh if she told them that she had once been born again herself. That sentence didn't make sense, but she knew what she meant. She would never forget that clean, washed feeling that had come over her when she knelt at the penitent-form. She wondered if it was something like Catholics felt after Confession. She had cried then too, but not very much. Not like the man next to her, whose body was shaking with sobs. Not in the heart-bursting way Andrew had cried when he stood near her that night at the Youth Rally.

Most of the friends she had nowadays knew nothing about that kind of experience. They probably didn't even know what a penitent-form was. They had read books, like *Elmer Gantry* and *Marjoe,"* where the whole evangelical thing was made to look like a con job which, of course, it often was. But not always. Even now, after having been through many phases very far removed from that teenage experience, she still had to say, not always.

The young man sitting next to her was singing fervently, his eyes closed, his right hand raised. She had done that herself, many times. She still remembered the ecstatic feeling, the shutting out of everything else, the sensation of being completely herself. It was a long time since she had felt like that. She looked again at the young man. She could tell he didn't even know she was there. Although he didn't look at all like him, for some reason he reminded her of Andrew.

Why was she thinking about Andrew tonight? It was years since she'd thought of him—consciously, anyhow. She had never even known him very well. Someone had told her he was married, and she wondered about that. Was it a solution for him, an escape, or just a measure of desperation? She thought again of that youth service at one of the big citadels so many years ago. Was that when her last church phase had ended, finally and forever? She had never realized it before, but perhaps it *had* ended there, or at least started to end. If that was true, though, what was she doing here now?

The prayer meeting, or whatever it was, finished, and the Great Salvation meeting began. That's what it was always called, a Great Salvation Meeting, usually sounding capitalized. She had been at Great Salvation Meetings led by young cadets where the congregation numbered no more than ten. She had also gone to some in huge halls with standing room only. That was the kind of service it had been when she had last seen Andrew.

The band was playing now, not a particularly good band but the kind that was put together by a zealous young amateur musician with more dedication than talent, made up of boys, and sometimes girls, who tried hard to stay together and in tune. You rarely heard of band members getting mixed up with drugs, or leaving home and living in communes, or worrying their parents, at least in the usual ways. Noreen envied those parents sometimes. Not that she'd had really big trouble with her children, not yet, anyway, though she was always almost morbidly conscious of the possibility. But Andrew had been a bandsman and if his mother had been comfortable it could only have been because she hadn't known. If there was anything to know at that time.

"Good evening, friends," the young officer was saying now, shouting, really. He had a light, almost high voice, not very well suited to public speaking. Many male officers had that kind of voice. It had made Noreen and her friends wonder, once. Certainly Andrew's voice had been deep enough. And he was big too: not particularly tall but broad-shouldered and muscular. "Those Martins can all take care of themselves," she had heard Richard say. He had gone to school with Andrew's brother Ron.

"For our opening song we'll sing Number 171. Number 171 in your Army song-book. The Band will help us and we'll have a real good sing." The officer gave out the words of the first verse and she knew he would line out the other verses too. She had never heard that done in any church but the Army.

> O wanderer, knowing not the smile
> Of Jesus' lovely face;
> In darkness living all the while
> Rejecting offered grace.
> For Thee Jehovah's voice doth sound,
> Thy soul He waits to free,
> Thy Saviour hath a ransom found,
> There's mercy still for thee!

He read the verses as if he had not done so dozens of times before. As he paused after each line, an Amen or a Hallelujah would ring out from one part or another of the small building. The young man next to Noreen shouted "Praise the Lord!" after the officer had finished the verse. Noreen sang as loud as the rest. This was the part of the service she liked best. She thought of Dinah's casual dismissal of Transcendental Meditation, EST, primal therapy, and all the other helping theories designed to bring people peace of mind and, incidentally, their founders a great deal of money. "They're all just a substitute for religion, Mom," she had said. "They're all a crutch." "A crutch can be pretty important sometimes, Dinah," Noreen had replied. "If something broken is healing, it's hard to get along without a crutch."

"Are you talking about a broken heart, Mom?" Dinah laughed. "Well, all right, I suppose you have a point. But *my* point is, if you have to have any of it, ordinary religion probably does the least harm. At least it usually doesn't cost as much."

The least harm. What a funny thing to say about religion. A broken heart. Had she been talking about a broken heart? Not really. Perhaps broken nerves, broken spirit, broken ideals, broken faith were more what she had in mind. Dinah didn't need a crutch, yet. She was young. But it seemed to Noreen that she herself had always needed one. She didn't have one anymore, had perhaps traded it in for a walking-stick that she used only on certain occasions. She smiled to herself, glad nobody could read her mind.

Noreen tried to remember when Richard had been to church last. Several years ago, certainly. And he had been so very active at one time. In fact, that was one of the things that had attracted her to him. Most of the boys she'd gone to school with went to church only when they were forced. Just like her own boys, except that she'd never forced them. Or her girls either. The young man next to her, he didn't look as though he'd ever had to be forced to go to church. Neither had Richard. Or Andrew.

Her mind was really wandering now. She thought of a magazine article she'd read a few years before. "What do you do when your church leaves you?" it was called. It had caused a furor at the time. The writer was a young Catholic woman who didn't like the new direction her church was taking. Noreen hadn't thought of Andrew when she read the article, but she thought of him now as she recalled it. Andrew's church hadn't left him, not in that way, for sure. Some outward trappings of the Army had changed over the years, but none of its basic beliefs had been tampered with. The word "deserted" sprang into Noreen's mind. What a lonely sounding word it was! But Andrew's church had welcomed him back the night of the Youth Rally. With open arms, as the officer had probably put it. Under certain conditions, of course.

The people who had stood around Andrew that night, as he knelt at the penitent-form in the big, crowded citadel had, Noreen knew, been genuinely prepared to forget his "record of sinfulness" just as they claimed their God would do. Just as they were willing to forget the sins of the drunkard, who seemed in danger of falling asleep on his knees, of the backslider, who "hadn't darkened a church door for five years," as he said himself. Or Noreen's own, for that matter. She knew she had

33

lots of them, certainly felt sinful enough, but she wasn't always sure what they were. Almost everyone knew what Andrew's were. Or was. It was only one sin, really, though probably repeated several times. There had been quite a scandal. Noreen couldn't understand how it was his mother hadn't found out about it. Perhaps, like the wives in three-cornered affairs, the mothers were always the last to know. She probably wouldn't have believed it anyway.

One of the bandsmen was leading the testimony period now. Noreen liked testimony choruses. They were so positive, so sure, so satisfying. Nobody was too bad to be forgiven and the people who stood up told about how forgiveness had come to them. Some were young, some old, some well-off, some poor, some former "sinners of the deepest dye" and others who'd "just dabbled around the edges of the pleasures of the world." They sang "Count your Blessings" and "There is a River" and "I am the Way, the Truth and the Life" and "Surely goodness and mercy shall fo-oo-ll-ow me, all the days, all the days of my li-i-i-ife." Noreen gave herself up to the singing. She wished, as she had often done before, that she could always, or at least often, feel the way she did at this moment.

Even so, the spell, or whatever it was, wasn't working as well as it usually did. Perhaps it was because she couldn't seem to stop thinking about Andrew. He had never been a close friend, just a casual acquaintance who seemed pleasant and friendly. She had been glad when he decided to go to the Training College, for she felt sure he'd make a good officer. He had the confidence, the sincerity, yes, even the faith that was necessary for such a committed life. Or he certainly appeared to have. She had thought once, naively, that faith would be the first requirement of anybody wanting to enter officer's training but she had discovered over the years that, in some cases, true faith had very little to do with the decision. Certainly not as much as emotionalism, a matter of "I'll do what you want me to do, Lord" promised in the fervour of a prayer meeting. This state of mind, for some, lasted only until the young officers found themselves in isolated settlements, far away from home, where they were expected to live on pitifully small salaries, where every move they made was watched closely by their congregations. Many dropped away, some to marry "outside," some out of bitterness and disillusionment, some simply because they weren't suited to the work. But there were always new recruits, undeterred by stories of the experiences of others, to take their places.

Noreen, like most people, had felt very sure that Andrew would last. He was no Johnny-come-lately to the Army, ablaze with the passion of a new convert. He knew what he was getting into, and seemed to have the strength and dedication for the job. She was glad when she heard he'd been appointed to Birchy Harbour, a place she knew well, where she had first discovered the Army, in fact. The people were friendly there, hospitable, and as tolerant as it is possible for people to be whose lives are interconnected and who have little contact with the outside world. She imagined him being invited out to supper, not only to the Salvationist homes but to some of the United ones as well. He probably wouldn't have been told the stories about how Millie Budgell was really Angus White's daughter—"spittin' image of 'un, you can see that" or about the danger of visiting certain families because they were TB A certain decorum had to be preserved with clergymen, at least at first. And there wasn't much TB around anymore, since the X-ray boat started calling in. Ruby Graves had been the last person in Birchy Harbour to die of it. Ruby wasn't talked about anymore now, at least not in a derogatory way. Death had made that pathetic little love affair respectable, and even rather romantic, especially after her married lover had erected a showy headstone to her memory.

With a start Noreen realized that the officer had almost finished his sermon. She had not heard one word he'd said, and he was obviously on his final point. He leaned forward, his arms outstretched.

"'Behold, now is the accepted time,'" he was saying. "'Now is the day of salvation.' Don't put it off, brother. Don't put off your soul's salvation, sister. Remember what Agrippa said to Paul: 'Almost thou persuadest me to be a Christian.' but almost is not enough, my friends. We all know that 'almost cannot avail.'" He started to sing, very softly:

> Almost persuaded, harvest is past,
> Almost persuaded, doom comes at last,
> Almost cannot avail,
> Almost is sure to fail,
> Sad, sad the bitter wail,
> Almost, but lost.

The congregation joined in, Noreen along with the others. Songs like this did not depress her as they had when she was younger. There was a haunting quality about them, an other-worldliness that took possession of her temporarily. She found the words and the melody soothing although, or perhaps because, she did not for a moment believe that there would ever be a Judgment Day or that "doom comes at last." Unless doom meant death. But there was another kind of doom, a kind that had nothing to do with whether or not one's name was written in "the Lamb's Book of Life." The doom that many people experienced while they were still alive, that Andrew had experienced.

When Noreen first heard the rumours about Andrew she couldn't, or wouldn't, believe them. Many male officers, even a few married ones, had had love affairs, or something resembling love affairs, with girls or women in their congregations; several female officers had fallen in love with young men in the communities they served, and a few had gotten pregnant. But a love affair, if it could be called that, with another man? She had scarcely heard of such a thing then. It was different now. Most of her present friends didn't consider homosexuality a sin anyore, certainly not as long as it didn't happen too close to home. But what did they consider a sin? Guilt was still in the vocabulary; sin was not.

The particular incident that caused all the trouble had started innocently enough. A Mr. Morton, a man much older than Andrew, had gone to stay with him in Birchy Harbour to help with a series of revival meetings. He was a religious man, a friend of Andrew's family, and it was generally felt that a young, inexperienced officer could use some support in his first year on his own. Noreen wasn't sure how the talk had started; she hadn't heard about it until months later. Some of the schoolboys were said to have "seen something" and later to have confessed that the young lieutenant had sometimes acted a little strangely with them. Finally, there was the evidence of the bedclothes and the false teeth. The small quarters held only one double bed. The false teeth incident should have been funny but Noreen had never felt like laughing about it. Neither had the people of Birchy Harbour, but for a different reason. Outraged, they talked about sending for the Mounties but finally compromised by writing to Headquarters in town. An investigation was held, Andrew admitted to everything, he was immediately dismissed and sent home. His mother was told that his health had broken down. It was strange—a big, strapping young man like her son.

After hearing about what had happened, Noreen had not seen Andrew again until the night of the youth rally. She had been young enough then to qualify as youth. Richard was still going to church at that time but had stayed home to look after the children. She went alone.

She had been surprised to see Andrew there, sitting with his brother Ron. He looked strange and uncomfortable without his uniform, which had suited him so well. He glanced at her, smiled and nodded, and she smiled back.

The officer in charge talked a lot about surrendering fully to Christ, living a life of holiness, giving yourself completely into His charge. "Don't try to make yourself better before you come," he urged. "Remember, 'if you wait until you're better you may never come at all.' Let Him take your burden. Let him take all your anxiety, all your care." Then the choral group sang softly, those angelic-looking girls who appeared as close to sainthood as it was possible for human beings to be. Noreen knew some of them didn't act like saints, but they were nice girls, most of them, trying to do their best. The girl who had picked her bonnet to pieces, she was a nice girl, too.

Even before she went to that rally Noreen had been tormented by doubts, doubts that she would hardly admit to herself, let alone to anyone else. Was there really a God? Most Salvationists didn't even go into this question; they assumed everyone believed at least that much. I'm not going forward tonight, she had vowed before the rally started. She knew she'd want to once the emotion thickened and she became conscious, as she always did, that something was missing from her life.

She did go forward, of course. When she knelt at one of the chairs that had hastily been placed in front when the penitent-form became crowded she felt the usual relief, the great sense of something heavy being removed from her shoulders. She stayed on her knees a long time, glad that nobody knelt and prayed with her. The officers were all very busy that night, and so she was left alone. She was never quite sure when to stand up but when the congregation started singing "Victory for Me," it seemed to be an appropriate time. She moved back to stand with a ring of people who had either been kneeling at the front or helping someone else who was there. It was then that she heard, and saw, Andrew, who was standing in the ring too.

She had never seen or heard a man cry that loud before. Come to think of it, she had never seen a woman or even a child cry quite that way, either. Andrew's shoulders were shaking, his eyes red and swollen; the sobs were dreadful and uncontrollable. "It's all right now, Andy boy," Noreen heard Ron say. "The Lord understands." But Andrew continued to weep, perhaps just a little more quietly. It seemed that he would never be able to stop.

One of the older officers, a visitor from the mainland who did not know any of the congregation personally, took over the prayer meeting then. He whispered to the pianist, and gave out the number of a song. He began to sing, slowly, softly, and soon almost everyone was singing with him.

> Jesus, my Lord, to Thee I cry,
> Unless Thou help me I must die;
> O bring Thy free salvation nigh
> And take me as I am.

As they reached the chorus, Noreen heard Andrew's voice, a little hoarse from the sobbing but still deep and true:

> O take me as I am,
> O take me as I am,
> My only plea Christ died for me,
> O take me as I am.

The bandsmen were scattered now, all around the hall, but one cornetist who was still on the platform picked up the melody:

> No preparation can I make,
> My best resolves I only break,
> Yet save me for Thy mercy's sake
> And take me as I am.

Andrew had stopped singing. He was crying again, quietly, hopelessly. A few officers, some of whom had trained with him, came and spoke to him, shook his hand, clapped him on the shoulder. He had obviously knelt for a long time at the mercy seat. What more could they do for him now?

Noreen had wanted to look at him but wouldn't let herself. She was afraid of what she might see in his eyes. Shortly afterwards she had picked up her songbook and her handbag. As she walked slowly down the street toward the bus-stop, she felt oddly disturbed, not at all at peace the way she usually felt after that kind of prayer meeting.

She had wondered about Andrew, that night and many nights later on, but she had never seen him again. She heard about his marriage and the births of his children. Sometimes, in the middle of the night, she would wake thinking she could still hear that awful crying.

"But they won't, will they?" she had said to Richard that night when she was trying to tell him about Andrew.

"Won't what?" Richard seemed preoccupied and deliberately uncomprehending, as he often did when she attempted to talk to him about serious matters.

"Won't take him as he is. You know they won't."

"How can they?" was all she could get out of Richard. But she was used to him and she knew that the words weren't as hard as they sounded.

She had continued to go to church, occasionally, when she felt the need of it. She was not sorry she had come tonight. But she knew that now it was time to go.

"Lay it all on the altar," the young officer was saying. "Remember, 'standing somewhere in the shadows you'll find Jesus, and He's the only one who cares and understands.' Don't put it off any longer, my brother, my sister. There's nothing the Lord can't forgive."

Is that really true, Noreen wondered, as she pulled her coat around her and buttoned it up. Supposing there is a Lord, is that really true? She glanced at the young man next to her. His eyes were closed, his lips moving in silent prayer. And even if it is, He only forgives the past. And only on the condition that you stop doing whatever it is. But perhaps she wasn't being fair to the Lord, whoever or whatever He was. Perhaps it was only those that called themselves His people who felt that way.

As she moved into the aisle, she looked toward the penitent-form. Although nobody was kneeling there yet, she had a feeling somebody soon would be. She hurried toward the exit, pulled on her gloves and began to walk quickly away. For a few moments she could still hear the music. Then she could hear it no longer.

The Summer Visitors

I had a letter from Nina this morning. She's about the only person in Newfoundland I ever hear from. Most of the people I know down there find it hard to write letters. Of course they haven't been properly educated, poor things. I thank my lucky stars I got out of there when I did. Father saw to that. He was working in Boston then. A lot of Newfoundlanders had to do that, go away to the States and work for months at a time. It was almost impossible to make a living in Newfoundland. My heavens, that must be nearly fifty years ago. Anyway, he made arrangements for me to come up and join him. I was only eighteen at the time, and green as grass. When I think about what the Americans must have thought of me I could die of embarrassment. The way I talked, for one thing. I remember a girl I worked with, Peggy, her name was. She used to make fun of me all the time. "'allo, 'azel, 'ow are you?" she'd say to me every morning. I could have killed her then but now, when I look back, I'm grateful to her. It didn't take me long to learn to speak proper.

Of course I couldn't help talking the way I did. What chance did I have, living in a little place like Cape St. Peter? The only thing that was plentiful in Cape St. Peter was rocks. A one-room school, that's all we had to go to, and half the youngsters didn't go at all. But I went. Father made sure of that. Poor Mother, I don't think she really cared all that much whether I went or not. She was sick nearly all the time, not cut out for life in a place like that at all. But Father, he was determined. "You got the chance to get a bit of learnin', you git it," he used to roar at me. "I never had the chance meself." And then, when I got older, all he wanted to do was get me out of Newfoundland. " I don't want you marryin' no Newfoundlander," he'd tell me over and over again. "I'm gettin' you out of here if it's the last thing I ever does." Funny, though, how he went back there himself, never really left it, I suppose. He always kept his house in Cape St. Peter, even after Mother died, and he was still only middle-aged when he went back there to stay. Perhaps he didn't care about himself. He sure was determined about me, though.

He didn't take it so bad when he found out I was going to marry a Newfoundlander. He always liked Max—knew his father and uncles in Bragg's Cove. That's only about seven miles from Cape St. Peter and everyone from all those little places always knew everyone else. And then, of course, I met Max in Boston. That made a difference too. He already had a good job in the factory by that time, with no intentions of ever going back to Newfoundland. He felt something the same as Father did about it. "Who'd want to live in that God-forsaken hole, Hazel?" he used to say to me. He's not a bit ashamed of being from Newfoundland though, the way some are. I've actually met people from there who pretend to be from somewhere else. "It's what you make of yourself that counts, not what you started with." I've heard Max say that so many times. Still, he never even wanted our two boys to visit there. They used to talk about it when they were kids. "What did you play at when you were small, Daddy?" they used to ask him. You know how kids are. And he'd say, "All I ever done was work. I never knew what play was." He didn't want to talk about it at all. Max really had it hard when he was growing up, more so than I did, really. I was an only child but he was the oldest of nine. He started fishing with his father before he was ten years old. "Sending a boy to do a man's job," he called it.

Strange, though, how he wants to go back every summer. He only started that seven years ago, when he retired. Before that he'd only get two weeks vacation and that wasn't much good. But the very first spring after he retired he said to me, "Hazel, let's drive down to Newfoundland this summer." I thought he was crazy. There's nobody left there belong to us now, only a few cousins. We sold off Father's house after he died. It didn't come into my mind that we'd ever be going back that way again. And now Max had to come up with this. I was worried about him driving all that distance. It was all right on this side, of course, but what would the roads be like down there? Probably not even paved. I was surprised to find out they even had roads. But Max had been talking to a friend of his who made the trip the year before and he said it wasn't too bad. It seems like they've made a lot of progress down there since they became part of Canada. Some people wanted to join up with the States instead. It's a pity they didn't, really.

I didn't have a clue who we'd stay with, but Max remembered his old cousin Bertha in Bragg's Cove and he got me to write her. The letter we got back was written by Bertha's daughter-in-law, Nina. I should have known Bertha wouldn't be able to read or write. Anyhow, Nina said we were welcome to come if we didn't mind putting up with what we found. Bertha was all crippled up, she said, and her house was old-fashioned, but there was a room for us if we wanted it.

The trip down wasn't all that bad. Some of the people we met on the ferry were raving about the scenery in Newfoundland; apparently they'd been there a couple of years earlier. "Ruggedly beautiful," that's what they called it. I've never been much for scenery myself. Give me comfort every time. I was surprised to find a few decent restaurants along the way. Nothing extra, you know, but passable. There was nothing like that in my day.

Well, you should have seen where we had to stay. I swear to God the house couldn't have been changed since before Max went away. Bertha still had no water or toilet in, she still used the old wood stove and the same old furniture she always had, even to the wash-stand in the bedroom with the splash towel behind it. She did have the electricity in, for a wonder. Nina lived next door, and her place was much nicer. Her husband, Gerald, is a great carpenter and he had it fixed up lovely. He put the water in himself, and they had a septic tank out back. They had nice modern furniture too, and a TV, though the reception is not very good.

We took to spending most of our time at Nina's and when we were getting ready to go home she said, "Why don't you stay with us next summer? We'll have a spare bedroom by then. Gerald is goin' to build a piece on the back of the house now when the work slacks off." We jumped at the chance and we've been staying there every summer since. Max gets a charge out of going out fishing with the men, picking bakeapples and blueberries, all the stuff he hasn't done for years. He likes it a lot better now that he doesn't have to do it. I'm not so keen, but it is a change. And the air is nice and fresh, although there's getting to be a smell from the fish plant.

The first few summers Nina was wonderful to us. Funny, although she's so much younger than I am, she reminded me of my mother. Her eyes are the same colour brown as Mother's were and she's got that look about her that people have when they're not very strong. You could really talk to Nina, too. I told her things I never told anyone else. She waited on us hand and foot, although I always tried to do my share. Some of the food was strange—they call margarine butter, for instance, and they use canned milk almost all the time. I put up with that for awhile, but then I found real butter and fresh milk at the new supermarket in Cape St. Peter, and after that I bought my own. Nina and Gerald used to laugh at Max and me with our own little butter dish and milk jug. They liked having us there, though. "It's so nice to have a bit of company, Hazel maid," Nina used to say. I tried to break her of that habit of saying *maid* but I never quite managed it. And her children, sometimes you could hardly understand what they were saying. I was always after them to come to Boston when they finished school. I know I thank God every night that I had the opportunity to go to the States when I was young.

Last summer was different. Nina seemed really altered. Gerald never did have a lot to say so we didn't see too much change in him. Of course Nina had been sick during the year, and perhaps that had something to do with it. Some days she'd hardly speak at all, and once or twice we even had to get our own meals. I believe she's having a hard time with the children. There's a bit of trouble with drugs in Newfoundland now, believe it or not. We never had any problems with our boys that way, thank heavens. There wasn't too much of it on the go when they were growing up. Anyway, I don't know if drugs had anything to do with it or not, but Nina's two children were certainly changed. They're not children anymore now. The girl, Veronica, was in university this year and the boy is planning to go to the Trade School in Clarenville. Nina is lucky she only had the two. There's still lots of big families down that way, but she always had trouble carrying children. I think she had six or seven miscarriages.

It's hard for me to get used to the idea of anyone from Newfoundland going to university. I don't suppose it's a patch on our colleges but they do get some kind of a degree. "You should come back to the States with me," I told Veronica. "You'd make something out of yourself there." "What makes you so sure everyone wants to go to the States?" she snapped at me. She's got quite a temper, that youngster. First when we started coming back she was a sweet little thing but she changed as she got older. After that, she back-answered me a few more times and one day the young fellow, Dennis, his name is, even did it to

43

Max when Max suggested he might be able to get him a job in the factory where he used to work. "It's just as well for me to go to work in the plant here if all I'm goin' to do up in Boston is work in a factory," Dennis said to him. "Anyhow, if I couldn't go off birdin' or snarin' rabbits every now and then I'd go foolish." I started to tell him about all the things he'd be able to do in Boston but he got up and left the room. I looked at Max. He'd never let our boys answer back like that, but I suppose he thought it wasn't his place to scold someone else's children. Nina just sat there and never said a word. She's got her hands full with those two. Herself and Gerald always did let them get away with murder.

A few weeks ago Max started talking again about going back to Newfoundland this summer. He always gets on to that right after Easter every year. So I wrote Nina, like I always do, although I hadn't heard from her since I got her card at Christmas. It was a long time before she answered but I finally got a letter this morning. It was the strangest letter I ever had from Nina. She hadn't been feeling well, she said, and she was afraid she wouldn't be able to put us up this summer. She hoped we'd understand. Poor thing. I wish I could get her up here and show her a bit of life, although I suppose it's almost too late for her to change her ways now. That's why I wanted Veronica to come, while she's young, like I was. I got Newfoundland knocked out of me years ago.

I don't know what I'm going to tell Max. He looks forward so much to going to Newfoundland every year. I'd just as soon go to Bar Harbor or Old Orchard if it was up to me. Poor Nina. I hope there's nothing seriously wrong. I guess we'll have to stay at the tourist home in Cape St. Peter. Bertha is not around anymore, she died three years ago. We thought about buying her house and doing it up for a summer place, but it would have been too expensive. The tourist home doesn't appeal to me but I guess it will be all right. Anyway, I don't see what else we can do now. I'll miss being with Nina, though. I really will.

Eva

Above all else, Eva found it hard to go back to work. She had extended the long week-end by two days, readying herself to face the inquiring eyes. And why should there be inquiring eyes? How could anyone at the library possibly know the explosive news that had come as such a completely unexpected, totally crippling blow to herself? Somehow she was sure they would all know, if not now, soon. Just as everybody always seemed to know everything in this town. And perhaps—wasn't this the final unbearable hurt?—they had all known for weeks, or even months. For months, Brian had said. At Christmas, then, when he had given her the new wool suit she had wanted so much.

She did her face carefully, wielding the lipstick and the makeup brush with a hand that scarcely shook at all. Her image looked back at her from the delicately embossed wall mirror that Brian had given her four, no it was five years ago. Other men might be driven red-faced to the lingerie counter on Christmas Eve, or try to make do with perfume, but that was not Brian's way. He had always made careful note of her preferences. Often, when he gave her something she wanted desperately, she could not even remember ever having mentioned it. Brian was almost psychic sometimes.

Her hair was all right. She was glad now she hadn't given in to her hairdresser's pleas to have it streaked. "Brighten you up," Patsy had said. "You'll feel like a million." But "Your Maker knew what he was doing when he gave you brown hair," was what Brian always said. "So don't fool around with it." And she hadn't. There was no grey in it; it was just a little faded. Still, it was right for her. She could see that now. She combed her bangs carefully over the left side of her forehead and flipped her back hair up around the brush the way Patsy had taught her.

45

She looked composed now, attractive, neat and efficient. "You don't have to tell me, it shows in your face," her mother used to quote. But she was determined that it wouldn't show in *her* face.

She was thankful that she would be doing the evening shift at the library, although it was one that she normally disliked. This way she'd only meet the staff as they filed out on their way home, most of them too concerned about their own plans for the evening to take any notice of her. It wasn't as if Gloria were around. Gloria knew her so well that she wouldn't be fooled. But she was still on holiday, her first trip abroad, with three other single friends. Eva had missed her keenly at first. Now her misery would not allow her time to think of anything or anyone but herself. She heard again, for the fiftieth time since he had uttered them, Brian's words.

"You know, Eva, you're not going to believe this." He had followed her into the bedroom and his half-joking tone had not prepared her for what he was about to say. She didn't even turn to face him but kept right on sorting the laundry into tidy heaps on the bed. Their bed.

"Damn that cigarette." Even though her back was toward him she knew that he had burnt his fingers again. She had once heard a psychiatrist say that only alcoholics burnt their fingers in that particular place. She remembered smiling at the time, for nobody but a rabid teetotaller could drink less than Brian did. And he was constantly burning his fingers.

Then, forgetting his sore finger, he plunged ahead recklessly and she was soon listening to a story that sounded like something from a confession magazine. She had stood perfectly still for the length of time it took him, holding a pair of Brian Junior's gym shorts in one hand and a yellow and red striped bath towel in the other.

Janie Abbott. Fancy having your husband taken from you by a girl with a name like Janie Abbott. It was such an apple-pie-ordinary sort of name. Come to think of it, Janie was an apple-pie-ordinary kind of girl, in a cool English way. Eva had met her almost a year before, when Janie first became Brian's assistant at the lab. Rather short and not particularly slender, she wore her wiry dark hair combed carelessly behind her ears. Her round, owlish glasses were continually slipping down over her nose and she wore no makeup, even at parties. Hardly the seductive rival most wives fear.

Those university parties. They had been an eye-opener to Eva. She had always thought of professors as slow-moving, preoccupied types living in a world of books and term papers, perhaps dozing over a chess-board or a game of Scrabble in the evenings. But the things that went on at the parties! Even now she could hardly believe some of the scenes she had witnessed with her own eyes—a lecturer in the English department, for instance, being passionately kissed by a history professor, and practically right out in the open, too. Both of them married, of course. And the absolutely filthy things they all said, well, nearly all. She and Brian had stayed on the fringe of the group. So, for that matter, had Janie Abbott.

Eva was a few minutes late at the library. Everybody had gone except Marian, who had her coat on and her purse dangling from her wrist. "Mr. Crane called," she told Eva as they passed each other. "He's coming in for the 1962 Parliamentary records. As if that was anything new."

Bob Crane was a tall, raw-boned young man with a spotty complexion and blue eyes that nearly always looked sore. For months now he had been patiently working on the records, one year at a time, going right back to 1949. "He's trying to overthrow the Government," Gloria was fond of saying, with that long, slow smile of hers that could never contain any malice. Eva pictured him in his street-level apartment near the waterfront. He never seemed unhappy, was always eager and polite, enthusiastic about his project, whatever it was. But Eva could see him plodding on, day after day, year after expectant year, until time ran out and he died obscure and unlamented. She gave her head a shake and called herself every kind of a fool as the hot tears in her eyes made her blink. She went to the cupboard in the inside room and took the 1962 volume from its place on the shelf. Coming out she almost collided with Bob Crane, who stood back deferentially and looked, for an idiotic moment, as if he were going to kiss her hand. She passed him the book and, head down, hurried back to the desk.

"Nice evening, ma'am." It was old Mr. Gallagher, touching an imaginary hat.

"Beautiful," she said briskly, although she knew the weather to be misty and chill. She slid around him to get to her chair. "Do you want the newspaper, Mr. Gallagher?"

"If you please, ma'am." What else did the old man ever want? She reached into the top right-hand drawer and drew out the folded newspaper. Keeping one hand behind him, Mr. Gallagher stretched the other one toward her.

Hiding the ugly diseased hand again. Gloria was sure it was a cancer, and Eva had to look away when he forgot and left it lying visible on the magazine table. Some of the patrons had complained about his handling the newspapers but, when Eva had forced herself to mention this to Mr. Drover, the Chief Librarian's only reply had been, "Cancer is not contagious, Mrs. Johnson." Now, paper tucked under his arm, old Gallagher shuffled back to his chair. For a moment Eva stared after him, thinking of the brave little yellow plastic flower eternally sprouting from his button-hole. Since she first began to work at the library she had watched him change from a shabby but upright old gentleman in a clean if shiny black suit to a slouching dodderer with last year's ashes still on his vest. Sometimes she was afraid that he would actually die in the library.

"He almost got the V.C. in the First War," Gloria, who had a knack for finding out things, had told her once. "And when the Queen Mother visited here last year the first one she asked after was Patrick Gallagher. He was presented to her husband when they were here in '39."

Sharply, she missed Gloria. For the first time since Brian had told her his news. Gloria, her soft brown eyes always compassionate —almost too much so at times, perhaps. Self-pitying, some people said, but Eva could not agree. Fragments of their conversations came back to her now. "Imagine, Eva, if you can, how terrible it is to realize that no man wanted to marry you. No man! It's a hard thing to face." She had said the words apologetically, looking sideways at Eva to see how she was taking them.

Eva had been embarrassed, but not as embarrassed as she would have been if another girl had told her the same sort of thing. Gloria wasn't being coy, hoping for reassurance or encouragement. She was simply stating a fact, and trying to accept it.

"You know that's not true. Remember that English Petty Officer you knew when the War was on, the one you saw every night for three months. Didn't he?"

"Well, he hinted at it, but he was killed, so that doesn't count. It probably would have been all the same if he had lived. Even so, there should have been others."

"But you had lots of boy-friends when you were young, Gloria."

"'When I was young.' You sound like my little niece. Let's stop being morbid—come on down and have a cup of coffee."

But Eve could not let the subject drop. "Perhaps, basically, it was that you didn't really want to get married yourself, Gloria. Your life was so full with your family, especially when your father was alive. Perhaps...."

"Now, psycho-analyzer, give it up. I'm not getting on any couch for you."

As they went downstairs to the staff room they talked of other things.

"Is the evening paper available, miss?" Eve looked up to find Miss Hartnell at the desk, her lips closed in a tight, thin smile, her hair immaculately neat in the style of twenty years ago.

"I'm sorry, Miss Hartnell, but Mr. Gallagher is using it. Perhaps when he's finished...."

"I'm not sure that I want to read it after him." The mouth was still smiling but it was like the painted smile of a stiff-faced doll. "Would you be kind enough to get the City Directory for me?"

Miss Hartnell found a place as far from Mr. Gallagher as possible. Eva watched her scanning the big directory, taking careful notes on the thick pad of paper she always carried. "What in Lord's name does that woman want with the City Directory?" Marian had wondered out loud more than once. "You know, Eva, she makes me nervous. Doesn't she you?"

She didn't exactly make Eva nervous, but rather awakened some indefinable emotion that always left her feeling rather sick. Where had she come from, this woman with her spotlessly clean but out-of-fashion dresses, her bargain basement shoes and her sharp, watchful eyes? Where did she live? Had she ever laughed spontaneously, kissed a man, hugged a child? What did she do when she wasn't at the library? She obviously had very little money, so why didn't she have a job? Oblivious of the fact that she was the subject of such concern, Miss Hartnell held the pencil tightly in her hand and wrote, and wrote, and wrote.

Eva thought of the nights when, after getting home from the library, she and Brian would sit around the kitchen table and drink cocoa and discuss the case histories of library patrons. Only she would do most of the talking. Brian would laugh and say, "It's a social worker you should have been, Eva, not a librarian. Let's get to bed."

But even in bed she would not be able to let the subject drop until Brian, his good humour finally worn thin, would say irritably, "Oh, come on, Eva, let's go to sleep. We can't change the world tonight." Or, in a more tolerant mood, he would throw his arm across her shoulders and say, "Come on, woman. What you need is a good fuck." And then she would laugh and pretend to be in the mood, even if she wasn't, as was usually the case. And as they lay entangled she would try to respond but all the while her mind would be racing from one subject to another, and she would be longing for it to be over so that they could talk again. Brian had never seemed to sense this. Of course sometimes she was in the mood, and then it was all right, but most of the time she was content just to lie beside him and feel his hand under her breast and listen to the deep, reassuring sound of his breathing. But she wouldn't be hearing that anymore, would she? That, like everything else, would be reserved for Janie Abbott now.

"'Scuse me, missus, who do you have to see about gettin' work here?" Before she even raised her eyes Eva's nostrils told her that it was one of the regular drunks, the fellow with the flattened nose, probably. He was fairly steady tonight.

"What did you say?" She straightened the blotter in front of her.

"I'd like to get a few days work. You know, movin' books around and that. I passed Grade Nine and I got a very good suit home." He tucked up the frayed sleeve of the long overcoat that was hanging from his shoulders.

"You'll have to see Mr. Drover about that," she said, still frowning down at the desk. "His office is at the new Centre. Try him tomorrow morning about nine-thirty."

"Put in a word for me, will you, missus? You won't be sorry."

Eve raised her eyes at last but now all she could see was his retreating back, and the bulge where the bottle rested. She hoped he would be out of the lobby before he started to drink whatever it was. A few nights before he had smashed a bottle of shaving lotion all over the stone floor out there and one of the janitors, poor Mr. Burton, had cut his hand badly trying to gather up the fragments of glass.

As a matter of fact, she had just finished telling Brian about that little incident when he had said in that light, understated fashion, "Eva, you're not going to believe this. Remember Janie Abbott? Well, she and I...." Only he hadn't said it that quickly. There had been a few pauses. And then the whole story came tumbling out.

"Some women want sex until it runs out through their ears." She remembered her mother's words on that dreadful afternoon when she and Eva finally had their "talk." It was just two days before the wedding and Eva had watched her mother almost physically screwing up her courage for nearly a week now. "But for most of us—well, for most of us it's just a bit of a nuisance that we have to put up with. Might as well be cheerful about it. A man's a man, as they say, though he's in a bottle."

Eva, her cheeks burning, had run down to the cellar for an unneeded jar of jam. She was convinced that sex for her would never be the obvious burden it was to her mother. And it had been almost as wonderful as she had anticipated. She loved Brian, she wanted no one else, this was the final perfect thing that brought them together. "You idealize it all too much," one of her young married friends had told her at the time. "Don't you ever feel—well, depraved, bad, like there's nothing you wouldn't do? Why, sometimes when I feel Jack's semen running down my thighs when I get up in the morning I want to shout it to the world. Don't you?"

Eva was shocked. She had never felt that way, and she was glad. The smell of the stuff made her feel uneasy, perhaps because it reminded her of the Cream of Wheat she had hated since childhood. And she sometimes resented getting all messed up with it, especially after a bath. "But even if you did feel like that you wouldn't admit it," an inner voice told her. She was good, though, at silencing inner voices. No, she did what Brian wanted, was always ready when he was, and she knew she pleased him. Occasionally she even had an orgasm herself. And that—well, that was indescribable. All sorts of pictures arose in her mind at such times that she was ashamed to think about afterwards. Yes, it had been very good at the beginning.

When had it stopped being good? She thought about that as she stamped a pile of magazines, flipped through the overdue box and checked the questions in the reference book. After Brian Junior. was born? Or the baby that died? She could point to no particular time or circumstance when what interest she used to have in sex began to decline. She had been comfortably sure that it happened to most couples; after all, one could hardly expect a caress from a husband to act as a kind of instant aphrodisiac forever. She prided herself that she never refused Brian outright but she was almost relieved when he didn't make the familiar preliminary motions. Or if she was menstruating, or could give some really good reason for saying no. When she read of other women's problems with husbands who had lost interest in sex she found herself wishing guiltily that Brian would lose just a little of his interest. Still, there had been a certain smug satisfaction in the knowledge that he still found her physically attractive. As he had, apparently, never stopped doing.

For even the night before he told her—stop, she commanded herself. Stop torturing yourself, for God's sake, woman. But she could not stop. Even the night before he told her he had reached for her, stroked her breasts in his gentle, loving fashion and pulled her toward him in that unmistakable way. A couple of lines from an old song flashed absurdly through her mind. "For a woman to a man is just a woman, but a man to a woman is her life." That wasn't really true, though, was it? For if a woman to a man was just a woman Brian should be able to make do with her instead of jacking up everything for the likes of Janie Abbott. He has been making do with me, she realized suddenly. And now he can't do it any longer.

She raised her head as a sudden burst of badly-suppressed laughter reached her from the round table out front. She frowned, about to shush the three regulars who had just assembled at their nightly meeting-place and then, with a shrug of her shoulders, she decided to let them be. She knew their faces by heart—the tall one with the tiny pug nose and the simpleton eyes; the short, seedy looking older man whose face was covered with moles and the fattish, sly-looking creature with the bold grin. They were harmless enough, most likely, and she felt the familiar emotion of pity for them more than any other. Three misfits, why shouldn't they find some consolation in one another? Brian knew about them, of course, and when the controversial law allowing homosexual relations between two consenting adults in private was passed he laughed over the paper and asked, "What are your three friends going to do now, Eva, play Eenie, meenie, minie mo?" She had spoken harshly to him then—why must he always be so flippant? And Brian had apologized and said very little for the rest of the evening.

She began to gather up reference books from the tables and put them back in their places. Not many students in tonight—not many any night now, since the posh new library had opened at the Arts Centre. "Why on earth didn't you apply for a transfer, Eva?" her friends asked in amazement. "Anyway, I don't see why they're keeping the downtown library open. It's just a hangout for bums."

"It's necessary," Eva always insisted. "The Centre is just too far away for people from the lower part of town. Not many of them have cars, you know. And they're not all bums. Besides, they wouldn't feel comfortable in that fancy place. Neither would I, to tell you the truth."

"Eva likes being with that kind of people," Brian would say. Joking. Of course.

"But a man to a woman is her life." Oh, for heaven's sake, she was humming that stupid tune. Was Brian her life? It certainly seemed so now but she had often thought that she could be happy alone. Or with Brian Junior. She had been ashamed of that feeling, and she didn't have it very often, but she could not deny that it had been in her mind more than once. It was nothing personal as far as Brian was concerned, she would tell herself. Sometimes she felt she didn't need any man. Men were so silly sometimes. They got sulky and childish and you had to placate them. They always wanted their own way, even while they were saying "Wherever you want to go." Worst of all, they were jealous of their own children. Brian had been, often. Always after her to go away for a weekend and leave Brian Junior with his sister. "You know Louise would be glad to look after him," he'd plead. "She loves kids." "Brian, we only have one child," Eva would remind him. "If we can't take him everywhere with us, what kind of parents are we?" She had always secretly resented the fact that Brian and the boy were not at all close, as she had imagined a father and an only son would be.

It was partly young Brian's fault, she could see that. He was never particularly interested in going places with his father, unless she was along. And Brian had never been the minor hockey league kind of father. Not that young Brian was that kind of child. He would rather read, or watch television, or play complicated card games of his own invention than go out with the boys. He played with girls sometimes, though.

I'll be able to leave my bedroom door open now, she thought. Brian had always wanted it shut, even though closed doors gave her a claustrophobic feeling. Brian Junior would ask her repeatedly to leave it open and then, when he came to them after a bad dream or in the early morning, he would find it shut. It had always irritated Brian, anyhow, to have the boy bursting into the room at all hours.

"Well, that should make it easier for all concerned now." She caught Bob Crane's eye and for one awful moment she was afraid she had spoken aloud. But there was no interruption in the swift movement of his hand, no flicker of new interest in his eye. She lowered her head

53

and pulled out a drawer, busying her fingers tidying the already neat array of pens and pencils. Young Brian would stay with her, and Janie and Brian would have a perfectly uncomplicated life. And she, Eva, what would her life be like? She remembered picking up Brian's discarded shirt the morning after he left and sniffing the perspiration-soaked armpits (such a heartening thing, the fresh sweat of a clean man) and she knew now, with frightening clarity, that she could not be happy alone. Or with Brian Junior. Another man? She almost laughed at the thought. *I don't really like men much.* It was the first time she had ever shaped the words to that thought, and though she didn't speak them it was as if she had. *I really don't, but I like Brian. I loved Brian. I still love Brian. Oh God, why does sex have to go and louse everything up? I could have got along very well without it.* But he couldn't. Oh, no. Brian couldn't. She had been a good wife to him, even sexually, or so she had thought. Could she help it if she wasn't wildly passionate? Like Janie? Well, he'll get his fill of it now.

She remembered her mother's words. *He'll get it now until it comes out through his ears.*

She made tight fists of her hands to drive back the tears. She looked at the clock. Time to dim the lights. She was sorry, really, that she had to go home. The library had become a haven. She wanted to go and lie down on that lumpy old sofa in the staff room, lie there in the pitch black and cry until she could cry no more. She didn't dare cry at home. Young Brian might hear, and didn't that child have enough to face?

After she had given the warning signal with the lights she watched the library patrons rise reluctantly to their feet. She knew they didn't want to go home either. Bob Crane placed the thick record book in front of her with his usual flourish. He grinned and whispered "Old Man Gallagher wants a date with you." But his shoulders drooped as he walked away from the desk.

She took a last look round. The man who had asked for a job had, unseen by her, wandered back and was sound asleep at the overseas newspaper table, his head resting on *The Sunday Independent.* She shook him gently and he woke up in terror. "I'm goin'," he muttered when he saw her. "Don't worry, I'm goin'." And he stood up and walked unsteadily toward the door.

Mr. Gallagher, bent and frail, nevertheless managed to look courtly as he passed her. "Good night, ma'am," he said, straightening just a little. He had his hat on now, and he lifted it gallantly. Then, very slowly, he started the long walk home. Miss Hartnell, her tight little smile fixed, had hurried out ahead of him, her pad of paper under her arm.

"He's going to die in here one of those nights." Gloria's words came back to her. The thought was not terrifying, as it once had been. It somehow seemed appropriate.

The three homosexuals, jostling each other but not talking, mumbled something as they passed her. Hold up your heads, she felt like shouting. Don't let everyone know how defeated you are, please.

She made one final round, pushing aimlessly at the chairs and straightening the magazines. Nobody left. She would have to go, too. She buttoned her coat and walked quickly out, carefully locking the door behind her. Then, her head held high, Eva followed the others into the street.

Wintergreen

Anna looked out across the Collar, its waters calm at last after the turbulence of the day. "The wind'll go down with the sun," her grandmother always said. But that was only one of the things her grandmother always said.

"Why do they call it the Collar?" Anna asked now. Ever since they came to Fowler's Cove she had wondered. "It's a harbour, isn't it?"

"The Collar is just the part where they moor the boats. There's hardly any harbour in this place anyhow, it's so open." Her grandmother was plaiting her coarse, grey-flecked hair and coiling it in a thick braid at the nape of her neck. "The men have always called it the collar, so I suppose there must be some reason. Hurry now, Anna, and get dressed."

Anna looked down at her heavy denim pants and striped top. "Oh, Gram, not again tonight," she wailed. "Where are you dragging me this time?"

"You know very well we're going to Aunt Rahab's birthday party. You were with me when Jean told us about it yesterday. Now, go and put on your blue polka dot. It's a good thing we do go visiting in the evenings, or else nobody in Fowler's Cove would ever see you in a decent stitch."

Anna dragged her feet slowly up the narrow white staircase. They'd been in Fowler's Cove for a week and it was the same every night, following Gram around from one house to another. First it had been Uncle Zachariah's, next Aunt Naomi's and then Cousin Beltashazzar's. "Where on earth did they all get the crazy names?" she had asked her grandmother early in the week.

"From the Bible, of course. The parents of that generation thought it very important for their children to have Biblical names. Now, by the time we came along it was all Violet and Florence and Albert."

"But John and Mark and Sarah and Lois are in the Bible, too," Anna had pointed out. "What was wrong with them?"

"Oh, they were too plain. They might have been mistaken for worldly ones."

"But you must admit Rahab is a strange choice," said Anna. "Why call an innocent baby after a harlot?"

"Shhh." Gram looked around as if someone might be hiding behind the couch. "As long as the names were in Scripture, that was all that mattered. Why, I remember one time the minister told me about a couple who...."

But Anna had fled out into the garden before her grandmother could finish. She just couldn't bear to hear the story of Pizlam Siv one more time.

She liked the garden. Now dressed in the approved blue polka dot dress, she slipped out there again. It had gone rather wild, for there was nobody to look after it now that her grandmother's house was vacant for so much of the year. The wildness suited this treeless place, Anna thought. Why couldn't they stay here in the garden instead of traipsing around again tonight? It was always the same—a scrupulously clean kitchen with the washstand in the corner and the big stove in the middle of the floor. The strange conversations Gram carried on with all those Biblically named creatures. The lunch that was served before they were allowed to go home—that was always the same, too—homemade bread, a tin of pink meat, thickly sliced and arranged on a platter, a dish of bakeapple jam and a can of pears or peaches tumbled out into a large bowl.

Her grandmother joined her and they started off. On their walk around the point they passed a group of shy children absorbed in their own special kind of play. It's all right for those little kids, Anna thought. Ideal, really. But how do the teenagers stand it here? I'd go stark, staring mad.

When they entered the large square kitchen of Aunt Rahab's house the old lady, starched white apron tied over her serviceable black dress, was in the rocking chair, her bony hands gripping the wooden armrests. A bottle of wintergreen liniment stood on a small table at her side.

"Well, well, Aunt Rahab, you're looking wonderful." Anna winced. Why did Gram always have to shout like that?

"Can't complain, Lily, my maid." Aunt Rahab's voice was dry, like the skin of her hands and face. "And this must be h'Anna." Anna had been in Fowler's Cove long enough to become accustomed to this pronunciation of her name. "I should have told them my name was Hannah and then they might have got it right, " she had whispered to Gram the first night. But Gram was not amused.

"Come 'ere and let me look at you," Aunt Rahab continued now, holding Anna at arm's length. "She's a lovely lookin' maid, Lily, but there's not much to 'er, is there?" She pinched Anna's slender arm. "Good thing she won't have to work on the fish flake, hey, Jean," and she turned toward her great-granddaughter, who was standing in front of the table with her parents. Jean was short and square and sturdy, with a round pink face that was more pleasant than pretty. She smiled now, and turned pinker than ever, but she said nothing.

Anna felt Gram's fingers on her back, prodding her into speech. Desperately she searched her mind for something to say. Finally she blurted out, "Have you always lived here, Aunt Rahab?" and then mentally slapped herself for such a vapid question.

Aunt Rahab, however, was apparently quite happy with it. She thought for a moment, said, "Oh, no," and then stopped. Anna prepared herself for a long, rambling story about Boston, such as she had heard from some of the other old people she had visited. But Aunt Rahab, her wrinkled face softening, only said, "We was up to Bonavista for a spell." Anna waited for her to say more, but the old lady just reached for the wintergreen bottle, uncapped it, and spread a liberal amount of the oil over her wrists and lower arms.

The evening passed slowly. Gram, of course, had a lot to say, as she did every evening, and she and Jean's parents found plenty to laugh about and exclaim over. Jean said very little, but every time Anna caught her eye she smiled. Anna knew Gram expected her to make conversation but everything she thought about was too inane to put into words.

Anna picked up the *Chase's Almanac* and looked for her horoscope. Then she checked her birthstone, her flower and her lucky number, all of which she knew only too well from other almanacs in other kitchens. Jean was setting the table, slowly and painstakingly; it was apparent that a great deal of preparation had gone into Aunt Rahab's birthday supper.

The old lady was nodding in her chair now, but Jean's mother gently shook her awake when the big round cake with its ninety glittering candles was placed in the centre of the table. Aunt Rahab blinked and said, "First time I ever seen a cake on fire," and then she reached for the wintergreen bottle again. Two flies buzzed near the cake and Jean, an anguished look on her face, tried to fan them away.

After Aunt Rahab had been helped to the big chair at the head of the table, everybody sat down. Anna, who didn't like tea, was given a glass of raspberry syrup that was not quite cold enough to be palatable. Feeling Gram's eyes on her, she made a valiant attempt to drink it all down.

"Make a long arm," advised Jean's father. Anna reached for one of the date squares. Like almost everything else on the table, they had been made by Jean. But just as Anna raised the cookie to her lips she got a strong whiff of wintergreen and a wave of nausea swept over her. She dropped the cookie to her plate.

When they were ready to leave, Aunt Rahab gripped Anna's hands tightly and said, "Have a good time while you'm young, my maid. I 'ad a good time when I was young." And Jean, still smiling, went to the door with them.

Anna and her grandmother were silent until they were almost back to the house. Then Anna said, almost to herself, "Poor Jean. She's never even been to St. John's."

"Is that a tragedy?" her grandmother snapped, but then, after a pause, she continued, "I've been trying to persuade her to come back with us for a couple of weeks."

One horrid little part of Anna shrank at the idea of showing Jean around, introducing her to all her friends, as Gram would surely have her do. Suddenly, she wanted nothing more than to be back home this minute, in her own airy bedroom, with the bathroom down the hall, and the streamlined kitchen where she had never seen a fly. Aunt Rahab's words, "Have a good time while you'm young, my maid," echoed in her ears and she shivered.

"Now I know you should have brought a sweater," Gram scolded but "I never want to smell wintergreen again" was all Anna said.

The Plan

As soon as Rita opened her eyes she knew there was something different about the day. Not special, no, that wasn't the word. Different.

The sun was bright, after a week of rain. Her room caught the light early; that was one of the reasons she had chosen it. The yellow walls made it seem brighter still. She closed her eyes again. Perhaps it was just a little too bright.

Well, can't lie in bed all morning, even if it is my birthday, she thought. She didn't want to get in the trap so many of the people in the cottages had fallen into. The trap of what is there to get up for?

She swung her legs out over the bed and put her feet to the floor, testing them. They felt fairly strong this morning. Some days they reminded her of the big rubber flippers divers wear. But they were all right today.

The floor felt cold and she reached for her pink furry slippers. That was one thing she had plenty of, slippers. They were such an obvious gift item. She'd probably get at least one more pair today.

By the time the kettle started to boil her toast was ready. She didn't like it too dark. No egg this morning, she allowed herself only three a week. But there was a fresh bottle of marmalade, her favourite brand, and she had lemon for her tea.

The mail came while she was drinking her second cup of tea. No bills this morning, that was a pleasant change. Three square white envelopes that indicated cards. And a small brown-wrapped parcel. Another pin, she decided. She had even more pins than slippers. She picked up the parcel and saw that it was from Janet. Even as a child

Janet had been very methodical. Rita could picture her going into the jewellery store well ahead of time, considering, frowning, and then wrapping and sending the package so that it would arrive exactly on the right day.

One of the cards was from Linda. It was sealed so there was probably a cheque enclosed. Linda had no time for shopping. Her teaching job, her night courses, her husband and three children all kept her very busy. But the cheque would be generous, probably far more than she could afford.

The second card bore a local postmark and the handwriting was vaguely familiar. Agnes Carter, who still lived in her old home on the other side of town. Rita rarely saw Agnes anymore; they had lost touch somewhere over the years. But they had known each other a long time, ever since school.

On the third card the name and address were typed, and the postmark said Florida. Who in the world did she know way down there?

Nothing from David, then. She smiled. He would probably phone later, perhaps even tomorrow when suddenly, conscience-stricken, he remembered his mother's birthday.

She went back to her tea, which was beginning to get cold, and turned the Florida card over in her hand, searching for a clue as to the sender. How Jim used to laugh at that habit of hers. "Why don't you open it, girl?" he would ask as she fingered a letter, a puzzled frown on her face. She could almost hear him.

Finally she did open it. The envelope was unsealed and the card slid out easily into her hand. It was a tall studio card, with a picture of a hen on the outside and the usual doggerel about a spring chicken inside. At the bottom, in black ink with thick heavy strokes, was written "All the best from Leila."

Her legs, quite strong this morning, now felt very shaky. Leila. She hadn't seen Leila for forty years. But there was so much to remember about Leila. And now the memories came flooding back.

Rita poured herself another cup of tea but before she got a chance to sip it the phone rang. "Good morning, Mrs. Noseworthyt," the bright voice said. As bright as my yellow walls, thought Rita. Brighter. And she made a mental note to have her walls done a paler colour when the painters came round again.

61

"Oh, hello, Mrs. Burke." Rita made her voice sound pleasant. "You're bright and early this morning."

"Oh, well, early to bed and early to rise, you know," Mrs. Burke said archly. "I was wondering if you'd like to come along to the Morning Coffee with me. You know, the one at St. Philip's basement. Grand place to pick up Christmas gifts."

Rita's right leg felt cold and she rubbed it as she spoke.

"Oh, Mrs. Burke, not Christmas already. Why, it's only September." Rita didn't want to think of Christmas. She remembered last year, her first Christmas at the Cottages, when every charitable organization in town, it seemed, had paid its annual Yuletide visit to the old people. Old! She'd only been sixty-nine then. She thought of that horrible night when a well-meaning young couple had driven her and Mrs. Soper from next door around the city to see the outdoor lights. What a conversation. The young people had spoken to them in very loud voices "convinced we have to be deaf" Rita said afterwards, and the remarks were of the type that many adults address to small children—"Isn't that *gorgeous*, ladies?" Rita had been supremely glad to get back to the cottage that night.

"It'll be here before we know it, Mrs. Noseworthy. And they serve a lovely cup of tea at St. Philip's."

I've got tea here, Rita wanted to say. And besides, I thought it was supposed to be morning coffee. But she didn't say it.

"No, thanks anyhow, Mrs. Burke, but I don't think I'm up to it this morning." Careful now, Rita, don't give her the impression you're sick or she'll be over with a bowl of fresh meat soup or one of her "shapes." "I'm just feeling a little lazy today."

"Well, all right, then." One thing about Mrs. Burke, you didn't have to worry about hurting her feelings. "There's a movie on at the auditorium tonight if you feel like dropping over. Give me a ring later on."

"I'll do that," promised Rita, already wondering how she was going to get out of it.

What's wrong with me? she asked herself irritably as she went back to her tea. Mrs. Burke only meant to be kind. Not for the first time she wondered what Mrs. Burke's first name was. Christian names were rarely used by the cottagers, and sometimes it was impossible to believe that Mrs. Burke ever had one. She might have been born Mrs. Burke, with her always-waved white hair, her sparkling spectacles, her silky dresses and her endless crocheting.

It suits her to be an elderly woman, Rita thought. No, that wasn't right. Elderly lady.

While I—what am I? Rita looked in the small mirror above the kitchen sink. She saw a small, square face, wrinkled now, and rather sallow. The brown hair, with the grey roots beginning to show through again, was surely much thinner than it had been a year ago. The hazel eyes were still bright, though they did seem to have shrunk in size. And those bags under them. You'd think I stayed up all night carousing. She turned from the mirror with relief, and put the kettle on again for fresh tea.

Almost against her will she picked up the card from Leila, and as she held it in her hand she thought of The Plan. Leila's plan. Was Leila remembering it, too? Was that why she had sent the card? But no, that was silly. Perhaps by now Leila was an elderly lady like Mrs. Burke.

Recklessly Rita put two more slices of bread into the toaster. My weight's pretty well down now, she argued with herself. And the diabetes—Dr. Lowe said himself it's nothing to worry about.

Impossible. Leila could never, ever, turn into a Mrs. Burke. Rita remembered her first meeting with Leila more clearly than she could recall the just-completed telephone conversation. She and Leila had shared a room at Mrs. Abbott's that first year they taught at the Central Primary School in Abbott's Harbour. "I don't run a boarding-house, you understand," Mrs. Abbott had told them primly at that first meeting. "But I've always considered it my duty to take a couple of teachers."

"Some duty," Leila had snorted later when they were alone in their room, she blowing the smoke from the forbidden cigarette through the open window. "Why, she locks up the bread in the night-time. Amy Forrestall told me that. As if anyone would want her old baker's bread, anyhow."

"Her macaroni and cheese was good, though."

"What there was of it," Leila went into a sudden coughing spasm. She had taken up smoking only recently. When she finally recovered she stood at the window and looked for a long time at the dusty road below. "I won't be here long," she vowed, and then turned to Rita. "Will you?"

63

"I hope not," said Rita, knowing that was what Leila wanted her to say.

They had both stayed at the school, and at Mrs. Abbott's, for two years. Then Leila had left to go to the university and Rita had married Jim. But they had been good years. Sometimes, thinking guiltily of her forty happy years with Jim, Rita remembered them as the best years of her life.

Leila was always getting some crazy idea or other. Like the Easter vacation neither of them had enough money to go home and Leila suggested that they hitch-hike, though of course she didn't use those words. Hitch-hike. In 1929. Rita smiled as she thought of what her blue-jeaned granddaughter would do with that bit of information.

The toaster popped and the bread was just right. Rita spread butter—not margarine, butter—thickly over it, and then heaped marmalade on top of that. She poured herself another cup of tea. I'll finish this one supposing the Queen phones, she promised herself. The sun was stronger now, and the little kitchen felt cosy and warm.

Leila had taught her how to do the Charleston, and had made her her first ice-cream sundae by dolloping strawberry jam from Mrs. Abbott's pantry, unlocked for once, over a saucer of ice cream from the shop down the road. They had lain awake at night planning their future. Leila was going to be something glamorous—she wasn't sure what—an actress, perhaps, or an artist of some kind, maybe even a famous singer. She sang first soprano in the church choir, though there had been a little trouble when Mr. Barstow found out she smoked. And Rita? More than anything, Rita had wanted to travel. India, China, Egypt—especially, for some reason, Egypt.

And you never got there, of course. You forgot all that when Jim came along. Silly little goose. All you wanted to do then was get married.

Well, we did get to England, Rita's other self argued back. And even Paris, just for overnight. And what does it all matter now, anyhow?

The last of the toast eaten, she felt very full. She gulped down her tea and carried the dishes to the sink.

Leila had travelled. Rita had received postcards from all over the world though never, oddly enough, from Egypt. Leila had married once, when she was about thirty, but it hadn't lasted long. And there had been no children.

Rita thought of David, and the thought was painful. Did all mothers love their sons best? Oh, she loved the girls, too, they were good, conscientious daughters, who never failed to invite her for Christmas, even though they lived far away. And both of them had offered her a home, though, to be truthful, they had seemed just a little relieved when she said no. David had asked her, too, of course, and Ruth had backed him up, but as much as Rita had wanted to accept his offer she knew it was best not to. What was there about David that made him so special? He wasn't a bit like Jim. He's like me, she thought, putting into shape something she had always known, ever since David was a toddler. Not in looks, but in just about every other way. His taste in books, his favourite school subjects, his dislike of competitive sports, his lack of physical co-ordination, his very opinions on things—all were remarkably like her own. Perhaps that's it, she thought. We like ourselves best, really, or any reflection of ourselves. And a good thing, too, seeing that's who we usually end up with if we live long enough.

She had been about forty when she realized, for the first time, that everything that happened for the rest of her life would be happening to her, not some vague figure of the future. She would remain in this body—the body would change—but she would remain in it until she died.

Reluctantly, Rita picked up Leila's card again. She examined it for a message. Surely after all this time Leila must have written a short note somewhere. She felt around inside the envelope for a slip of paper. But there was nothing.

She knew now that she could no longer avoid thinking about The Plan. Whether Leila had intended that she should or not, she had to. Although she had not consciously thought about it for years it had probably been at the back of her mind all that time, just needing something sharp and unexpected, like Leila's card, to bring it to the surface.

It was during that first winter in Abbott's Harbour that Leila had first broached it, on one of those dreary doldrum January evenings when Christmas holidays are over and spring is light years away.

"Wouldn't you hate to be old, Rita?" Leila was sitting on the metal bedstead, a favourite perch of hers. "I mean, is there anything worse?"

"Yes," Rita had said. "Being dead." She was just learning to be flippant.

"Do you really think it would be worse to be dead? At least you wouldn't know about it. There'd be no you anymore, would there?"

Rita shivered. She did not enjoy this kind of conversation.

"To tell you the truth, I'd rather not be old *or* dead." She walked restlessly to the window and looked out into the gloomy night. "Can't we talk about something else?"

Leila was quiet for a moment and then she said, "What would be the use of being alive if you were like Mrs. Chafe? Tell me that."

Mrs. Chafe was Mrs. Abbott's mother. She had been lying helpless in a downstairs bedroom since a stroke had paralyzed her a year before. She could neither speak nor move.

"Do you think she knows anything?" Rita asked. Mrs. Chafe's eyes were open most of the time but they didn't seem to focus.

"Mrs. Abbott certainly thinks she doesn't. She treats her like a sack of potatoes." Leila jumped down from the bedstead and joined Rita at the window. Rita said nothing. "Better if Mom was gone clear of it all," she had heard Mrs. Abbott say briskly as she sponged off the unresisting figure in the bed. "She don't know she's alive, anyhow."

More than once Rita had silently prayed that Mrs. Chafe could not hear what her daughter was saying. But prayer—that was another thing. Until that year she had believed implicitly that there was Someone Up There, but now she wasn't at all sure. Leila was quite convinced there was no one.

"Stands to reason, Rita. We're just animals like all the others. Everything else is a pipe dream."

Rita wanted desperately to believe in God, or at least Some Power, but yet she didn't want to believe it if it wasn't true. She remained suspended somewhere between belief and disbelief and, as a consequence, was probably less content than those who were convinced one way or the other.

"Don't you think Mrs. Chafe would rather be dead than the way she is now, if she had the chance?" Leila continued. "I know I would, in her place."

They talked and argued far into the night, until Rita finally admitted her agreement with Leila and then, just as they were preparing for bed, Leila sat down beside Rita and said: "Tell you what, Rita, let's make a pact. Let's promise each other that if we're still alive at a certain age—say seventy—we'll take sleeping pills and end it all. Who'd want to live past seventy, anyhow? There's nothing for anyone after that."

Seventy seemed a long way off to Rita, and Leila's plan had a certain attraction. Still, she couldn't give in without an argument. "Suppose we don't want to when the time comes?"

Rita could almost see the impatience running through Leila's thin body. "Lord, nobody's going to *hold* you to it. But I can't imagine *not* feeling like it. Can you, now, really?"

"Somebody might need you."

"You'll never shake off the Christian ethic, will you, Rita." Leila had picked up that phrase in something she'd been reading, and she used it often. "All *right* then, if someone really needs you, you're absolved. But otherwise—a quick dose and a nice dignified end. No vegetating away into something like Old Lady Chafe."

They had joined hands then, and solemnly agreed. A few minutes later they were sleeping soundly.

After that night Leila had referred to The Plan only once or twice, briefly. When they finally left Abbott's Harbour Mrs. Chafe was still alive, "if you can call it alive," said Leila, and Mrs. Abbott was still telling all who would listen that "Mom is a nawful care to me, my dear, a nawful care. The messes I've had to clean up, you wouldn't believe."

Rita jumped and looked around her own cheerful kitchen. She had been far away, in that small, chilly bedroom at Mrs. Abbott's, and it jolted her to come back.

She heard knocking. Perhaps someone had been at the door for a long time though she could not remember hearing the bell ring. She smoothed her hair, did up the last button on her wrapper and walked out through the hallway.

"Good morning, Mrs. Noseworthy. I trust I'm not calling too early." Mr. Allen stood on the step, the round little clergyman who lived in one of the cottages and was forever trying to interest the rest of them in his "tour of the Holy Lands." He would apparently get a free trip for himself if he got enough others signed up. Mrs. Burke was going and she had told Rita earlier that she would be sending Mr. Allen to her. He looked everywhere but at Rita now, embarrassed because she was still in her night clothes.

"Oh, Mr. Allen." She strove to find the right words. "Could you come back this evening? I'm involved in something right now that I can't leave."

"Certainly, Mrs. Noseworthy, whatever suits you." He seemed relieved, probably feeling that he would do a better selling job if she were properly dressed. "I'll just leave a couple of those pamphlets with you, if I may. And think it over, will you? The cost is very reasonable."

She closed the door and stood a moment leaning against it, the knob still in her hand. Why didn't I get it over with? All it needed was a firm, gentle no. For of course she didn't intend to go. She couldn't afford it, for one thing. And there was something about those words "The Holy Lands" that had always repelled her. They sounded so unctuous, like the clergymen who used them, who seemed to feel that there was a special virtue in travelling there that was not found in any other place.

She turned over one of the pamphlets. Surely that was a picture of Egypt. But Egypt wasn't "The Holy Lands." Or was it? Perhaps it was just thrown in as an extra.

Fancy me walking through the streets of Cairo between Mr. Allen and Mrs. Burke. She giggled aloud. Well, who would you expect to be between, Rita, Joanne Woodward and Paul Newman? Just who do you think you are?

I'm an old lady. It was draughty here in the hallway. She adjusted the thermostat and then put her hands over the register, waiting for the warm air. No, not an old lady. An old woman.

She went back to the kitchen and fiddled with the radio knobs but could find nothing she wanted to listen to. She sat down at the table again. The remnants of her breakfast were still there. Well, I can see this is going to be a do-nothing morning. She put her feet up on the chair opposite and just sat.

I'm not needed, am I? Janet and Linda and David would cry if I died, but they'd soon get over it. The grandchildren don't really know me very well. No one really knows me very well.

Who had ever known her very well? Jim, of course; for a long time after his death she could hardly believe she was not dead too. And who else? There was only Leila. She had never had many close friends.

For the past six months she had been helping slow learners at the primary school nearby with their reading. It had been Mrs. Burke who got her into that, when she found out that Rita had been a teacher "for two years fifty years ago" but Mrs. Burke wouldn't listen to her.

"You're just the type, my dear," she had said, and before Rita knew it she was back in the classroom twice a week, a very different kind of classroom, guiding the children's halting progress through their insipid little books.

She quite enjoyed it, really. One little boy looked very much like David at his age, though David had always been bright. But she knew they would not miss her. Maybe ask for her once or twice and then get to know the somebody that Mrs. Burke would find to replace her.

Her father had died quickly, of a heart attack, her mother slowly, of cancer. With Jim it had been a combination of ailments, and near the end he had no longer been her Jim at all. Wasn't Leila's way better, to go when you were ready, quietly, gracefully, without the indignities that a long illness forced on you?

I'm as ready as I'll ever be, she thought. And I've even got the pills. Dr. Lowe had given her a prescription last year after that minor surgery, when she'd had trouble sleeping. There were a good many left.

I'd better find out how many it takes. Wouldn't want to end up in hospital with my stomach pumped.

She was surprised to find herself so matter-of-fact. She didn't feel any more spiritually inclined than she ever had nor, for that matter, any less so. She had once believed that wisdom and serenity came with age, but she felt just the same about most things as she had for years. There was no sense of wholeness. It was as if she was still looking for something to complete things.

Maybe death did that. But then, how would you know? Was there a magic moment—sounds like Lawrence Welk—just before the veil dropped, when everything fell into place? She had not noticed it with the few she had seen die.

I'll do it here, in my own bed, she thought. She had once heard of a woman who drove off to a park to take her pills. But that would not be necessary for her. Deaths were commonplace at the Cottages. There probably would not even be an autopsy.

She looked in the fridge. Two pork chops and a cauliflower. She would have them for lunch, with a nice thick cream sauce over the cauliflower. And then she would go for a walk.

The rest of the day was much like any other. The world was not preparing to mourn because Rita Noseworthy was leaving it. But neither did it look any more beautiful than usual. It was just the same.

She went to the small supermarket on the corner and bought two nice ripe bananas and a can of Pepsi. She hadn't drunk Pepsi for years. Gassy. But it didn't matter now.

When she got home she made herself a sandwich out of sliced tomato, cheese and ham. Now there was very little left in her refrigerator. That was as it should be.

After supper she took a warm bath, put on her best nightie and the long blue robe Janet had sent her last Christmas. Still no call from David. He had probably forgotten completely.

She turned on the television and curled up on the chesterfield, bananas and Pepsi on the table at her side, to watch Carol Burnett and Harvey Korman do their imitation of an old couple. She had often felt tempted to write them and complain about their exploitation of a minority group. But were old people a minority group? Certainly not around here. Anyhow, tonight she didn't care.

Am I really going to do it? Really? She had always been a physical coward, not at all like Leila, who had jumped over whole flights of steps when the whim took her, dashed madly around Abbott's Harbour on the old bicycle she had bought and even dived off the high board at the swimming pool in the Park. But Rita had always taken care that she wouldn't hurt herself.

Isn't that what I'm doing now, she thought, as Carol made one of her cracks about Harvey's loss of virility. Still protecting myself against possible hurt? Wanting everything easy? Well, why shouldn't I? There's no great virtue in things being difficult.

Harvey was shuffling across the floor, bent almost double, when Rita heard the first ring of her doorbell. Oh, God! Weren't they going to let her do this in peace? I won't answer it, she promised herself. But then it rang again, and yet again, more shrilly each time, it seemed.

I'll have to go or they'll be beating the door in to see if I'm dead. She almost laughed at the thought. By the time she reached the little hallway she could see that the door was slightly ajar, and she could hear voices behind it. With a sinking heart she recognized Mrs. Burke's strident tones.

As she was about to put her hand on the knob the door was flung open, almost knocking her down, and several voices chanted loudly:

> *Happy Birthday to you,*
> *Happy Birthday to you,*
> *Happy Birthday, dear Rita,*
> *Happy Birthday to you.*

And then Mrs. Burke, alone, continued with

> *We hope you live to be a hundred,*
> *We hope you live to be a hundred,*
> *We hope you live to be a hundred,*
> *A hundred years or more.*

"What a thing to wish on poor Rita." The low, controlled voice sounded somehow familiar, and Rita recognized Agnes Carter on the fringe of the group. Where in the world had she come from?

The others were all Cottage people—besides Mrs. Burke there was the Reverend Mr. Allen, the two sisters from Number 37, and several others that Rita knew only by sight. Mr. Allen carried a huge thickly-frosted birthday cake, and Mrs. Burke had a large bowl which looked as if it might contain one of her famous shapes. The younger of the sisters from 37 had a big plate of sandwiches and another woman clasped a square cookie tin to her bosom.

Rita looked down at the long blue housecoat. Mr. Allen must think she lived in night clothes. "But how did you know?" she gasped, carried along in the midst of them as they all hurried to the kitchen to stow away the food.

"Well, I met Mrs. Carter at the coffee party this morning—such lovely eats, too bad you missed it—and we soon found out we had a mutual friend. One thing led to another and before we knew it we had this little gathering planned." Mrs. Burke beamed at everybody and then started giving directions, as if she were in her own cottage.

The evening passed pleasantly, once the first stiffness had worn off. More pleasantly, really, than Rita would ever have believed possible. Mrs. Burke—"now, Rita, you really must call me Violet"—was, of course, in charge. Violet. What a singularly inappropriate name. Nothing shrinking about her. But she had come out of the era of the Violets, and the Pansys, Daisys and Lilys. Anyway, how could Mrs. Burke's mother ever have realized the kind of woman her helpless little baby would turn out to be?

Not that she was so bad, really. Sitting on the chesterfield with Agnes beside her, Rita was struck anew by the efficiency of Mrs. Burke. She organized everyone, but perhaps this was just because she was so well-organized herself. And she was thoughtful, you had to admit that. She had even brought a stiffly starched tablecloth and napkins, and a few extra teaspoons.

After they had all gone Rita stood alone in the hall, marvelling that the evening had not been the ordeal she would have anticipated if she had known about the party in advance. Mr. Allen had shown his slides of the Holy Lands, and Egypt was included. He was quite nice, when he forgot to be pompous. Mrs. Burke—Violet—had coaxed them all into charades in imitation of a popular afternoon television program and Rita, who had always been fond of acting when she could forget to be self-conscious, enjoyed them. But more than anything else it had been good to see Agnes again. A bit heavier, a bit less supple, a bit slower in her movements, Agnes had not really changed a great deal over the years. Why had they ever lost touch?

She moved back to the kitchen, immaculate after Mrs. Burke's washing-up. I think it's cleaner than before she came, Rita thought. She looked into the mirror and saw what David used to call "a leftover smile" on her face. It was a long time since she had seen herself smile.

"Come and see us soon," Agnes had whispered as she was leaving. "We'd love to have you."

We? Rita felt stupid. Who was we? Agnes' husband had died many years ago, long before Jim even, and their only daughter Elizabeth was in England. Agnes must have noticed the mystified look on Rita's face for she laughed and said, "Mother and me."

"Your mother's still living?"

"Indeed she is, ninety-four and smart as a bee. Makes me feel like a youngster."

She remembered Mrs. McLaren well from her school days, when she would often go to the big house after school with Agnes. Mrs. McLaren was rarely ironing or cleaning, like the mothers in the other houses Rita visited. She might be writing a letter, or entertaining at afternoon tea, or talking to a friend on the new telephone. But there was always a warm welcome for Rita, and usually a piece of cake or a hot scone.

When she went into the bathroom to brush her teeth Rita noticed the bottle of pills where she had left them earlier. A glass stood beside them. She looked at them for a moment and then turned and quickly left the room.

Not tonight. There was plenty of time. David still hadn't phoned. He would probably remember tomorrow. And she had made another appointment for Mr. Allen to come and talk about the Holy Lands trip. Not that she had any intention of going.

When she got into bed, the soft light from the lamp subduing the yellow of the walls, she was comfortably tired but not really very sleepy. The events of the evening made pictures in her mind—Mr. Allen acting out a chocolate chip cookie, one of the women from Number 37 moving in jerky rhythm as she listened to a record, Mrs. Burke carefully lighting the seventy candles. And then her mind reached back to the afternoon when Leila's plan had driven everything else from her mind.

If someone needs you, you're absolved. She remembered Leila's lightly spoken words. Absolved. Absolution. It all sounded so mystical, so unreal.

Walking

She steps through the doorway, turns to lock the door, tries the knob once. Then she walks down the steps and toward the sidewalk. Her loose black coat hangs well below her knees; the grey slacks showing beneath the coat are turned up around the ankles. Her shoes are black, with laces and low heels.

She walks in the middle of the sidewalk, a grey purse hanging from her left shoulder. Her dark hair, with its few strands of grey at the front, falls loose to her coat collar. She wears a bright red beret, pulled slightly to the right side of her head. In her right hand she carries grey gloves that look too shiny to be real leather.

She looks neither to the right nor to the left. A young man, almost running, passes her on the outside of the sidewalk. He glances at her; she does not look at him. A man and a woman, arms linked, nearly collide with her before they move to one side.

With her index finger she rubs the skin behind her ear. She looks at the finger, then lets her hand drop to her side. A black cat, white at the throat, rubs itself against her legs. She pays no attention.

Her eyes are brown, with flecks of grey around the irises. They look larger than they are because she seldom blinks. Without pausing or looking in either direction she crosses the first intersection. A red Toyota, crowded with young people, swerves and almost hits the edge of the sidewalk. The driver sticks his head through the open window, yells and shakes his fist at her.

Still looking straight ahead, she steps onto the opposite sidewalk. The street begins to slope here. Her feet in their plain black shoes adjust to the change, her steps becoming a little shorter. There are holes and bumps in this part of the pavement; she avoids them without looking down. When she passes the green house with the peeling paint she stops, turns her head and stares at the closed front door. Almost immediately she lowers her eyes, her shoulders twitch, and then she is again looking directly ahead.

At the bottom of the street she turns right. A men standing in a doorway on the opposite side of the street looks at her and opens his mouth. He does not speak. An old woman with long grey hair leans through the open window above him and calls, "Here, Ringo, here, Ringo." A brown and white beagle barks and bounds toward the front door of the house. The man pats the dog's head and lets him in. The woman in the black coat is still looking straight ahead as she walks. Her body jerks when she hears the dog barking. The strap of her purse slips down her arm; she pushes it back to her shoulder again.

She crosses the street, turns left and walks down the hill without altering her pace. She passes a crowded parking lot. When she reaches the wrought-iron fence surrounding the large cream-coloured house she stops. The house has brown trim and a coloured brick front. It's much larger than the other houses nearby. The lawn is thickly sodded and smooth. There are two flower beds near the house; the flowers, red and yellow and purple and pink, are all the same height.

The woman stands near the open gate. She wraps her hand around one of the iron fence-palings. She grips it so tightly that all the colour leaves her hand and it turns a chalky white. As she stands there two women look at her and then at each other before they pass in though the gateway.

She takes her hand away from the fence, moves it to her head and pulls off the red beret. She steps through the gateway, stops, and steps back. Two teenagers standing on the verandah laugh nervously. She passes the beret through her fingers a few times, then walks slowly toward the corner of the street. Her steps quicken as she walks back along the sidewalk. She does not look back toward the big house. The red beret dangles from her hand.

A Long and Lonely Ride

If I were on the train the wheels would say, "Run away, run away, run away." That was one thing about the train. You could always fit words to the sound made by the wheels. On those trips to Thursday Bay years ago, the wheels would say, "Summer's here, summer's here, summer's here," and then, more sombrely, when summer was ending and we were going home, "Back to school, back to school, back to school." The trains don't run anymore, not for passengers, anyhow. We have buses now, big road cruisers, and the wheels don't say anything at all.

I'm so desperate to get away I can hardly wait for the bus to start. Yes, desperate is not too strong a word for it. It's the only one for the way I've been feeling. One day last week I felt if I had to cook another dinner I'd go quietly crazy. Or maybe not so quietly. Screaming would help, but it scares people, and I'm not alone very often. On Friday night I frightened everyone to death by lying on the chesterfield staring into space, not reading, not watching TV, not doing anything. Not even talking. That was the thing they all found so hard to understand. I talk such a lot.

They all encouraged me to get away and I forced myself to take three days off. Three days. Not very long. But the preparations were great and the guilt was heavy. The other few times I had left them it was always for a conference or a meeting, something legitimate like that. But now I don't even have an excuse. "Don't be a martyr, Mom," said Beth when I tried to tell her how I felt. It's easy enough for her to talk.

"It's your own fault," I'm told, over and over again. And I suppose it is. But that doesn't make it any easier. Harder, if anything.

I've always hated leaving, anywhere, anyone. Everything will surely change for the worse while I'm gone. How egotistical we women are, forever thinking nobody can get along without us. "We're not babies," said Beth. "Mom, I'm twenty, you know."

I know, I know. And I'm forty-five. Isn't that a horrible age to be? When Mark was in high school he had to write an essay on the topic "When I Am Forty-Five." I remember it well. We were going together, even then. Were we ever not going together? It was a good essay he wrote, still home somewhere. He wasn't as neat then as he is now, and of course the pens were different, so there are a few blots on it. He and I were both famous for blots. But we've never blotted our copybooks, no sir. We're clean, almost painfully so. We don't drink, we don't smoke, we don't play around. The psychiatrist that Nigel was going to during that dreadful phase last year thought this might be part of his trouble.

"You're hard people to live up to," he said, looking at Mark. Then he turned to me. "Nigel just has to break those apron strings," he said.

My God, how do you know what's right? I don't think I've pampered Nigel, but I suppose I have favoured him. "You should have had the boy before the girls," he told me once. As if it were my fault. It was difficult for him, a boy following two girls. He never liked rough play, shied away from competitive sports, and when he was little he had more girl playmates than boys. What was that Mark had said to him once? "Sometimes I think you *are* a girl." It wasn't like Mark to blurt things out like that.

He had always been so pleasant, Nigel had, until this year. What does sixteen do to a boy? He's grown so much that he's almost grotesque. And all that hair. Then there was the trouble at school, principal phoning Mark and me—"His eyes look so troubled, Mrs. Johnson." I should have known then. "A few months ago I thought I'd have to put Nigel in hospital," the psychiatrist told us that day. Mark and I looked at each other. We'd known about the antidepressants but we had not realized it was that bad. It's very sad, the things you don't know about your children when they get into their teens.

"He seems better now, though," the doctor continued, sounding slightly cheerful for the first time since the beginning of the interview. He buttoned the jacket that he had been busy unbuttoning earlier. His hands were never still. He should see a psychiatrist, I thought, and almost laughed out loud. The doctor stood up and we knew it was time for us to go.

Nigel does seem better now, less sullen, more communicative, but a line has been crossed. He smokes heavily, though we don't let him do it in the house. "That's a mistake," I've been told. "He'll just do it outside." Well, he does it outside anyhow, doesn't he? We know he does. And he knows we know. He's got that cough already. "The criminal with the hacking cough," I call him sometimes when a bit of the old rapport comes back. His clothes all smell of smoke and stale tobacco, his fingers are yellow from nicotine, his pocket money disappears quickly. He's sixteen now, and thinks he's a man.

"Smoking," laugh my friends. "If that's all you have to worry about." "Do you *want* to get lung cancer, or what?" I asked him one day. He shrugged. He shrugs a lot. "I don't mind dying young," he said. "Well, I mind you dying young," I snapped, anger covering my anguish. "And don't you know that death by lung cancer is one of the most horrible you can have?" He shrugged again.

"If that's all you have to worry about." What nonsense. Does the fact that a person smokes automatically ensure that he doesn't do what we euphemistically call "other things"? That's too much like the old suspicion that the non-smoking, non-drinking, non-swearing churchgoer must be secretly guilty of a far more dreadful vice.

I know he's had a few drinks. What boy hasn't, today? "Everyone can't be like you and Dad, you know," he said one night. I know everyone is not like us. I have an obsession about alcohol, because of my father, I suppose. Some people can handle it, the rational part of me says, but I don't believe it, really. Not in my heart. Still and all, it was the night Nigel told me he smoked marijuana that I hit bottom.

I don't know why I was so upset. I'd suspected anyhow, and I suppose he'd be an oddball if he didn't do it. I had never considered marijuana as dangerous a drug as alcohol. But I cried and cried that night, uncontrollably, surprising Nigel, who had thought I'd take it calmly. No matter how tolerant I was of others, I've always had the almost hidden conviction that those things happen to other people's children, not mine. And that somehow it's through some fault (or weakness?) of the parents. In the same way I've felt it's all right for other people to have affairs, nervous breakdowns, tantrums. But not me. Never me. It goes even further, really. Children who've never had a chance, who've grown up in poverty and deprivation, they're the ones who take drugs and get into other kinds of trouble. Who can blame them? Or at least children of alcoholics, or broken homes, or something. I can feel genuinely sad for such families, even cry, but there's a small amount of justification, of satisfaction even, in the cause and effect. Those things are not supposed to happen to people like us, people who always do the right thing.

"I've wanted to tell you for ages, Mom," Nigel said that night, looking at me out of those blue eyes that might have belonged in an angel's face. "I don't like keeping things from you."

"Will you tell your father?" I asked, not looking at him.

"You know I won't. He'd go cracked."

What about me? I wanted to yell. I'm not supposed to go cracked, am I? "You're the best mother," Jan used to say, after unloading all her cares. Sometimes I wish I were the worst. They probably only tell me to ease their own minds, anyhow. And I'm left with a burden that I don't want and can't decide what to do with. "Bear ye one another's burdens." That's in the Bible. I know a lot of things that are in the Bible. I wish I had someone to bear mine.

And even so, I'm pretty sure there are still lots of things they *don't* tell me. All of them, but especially Nigel. I shiver sometimes when I think of what those things might be. "My son's gay and that's okay." I saw that in a magazine picture once. On a button a middle-aged woman was wearing. Did she really think it was okay, I wondered at the time. But if it wasn't, what could she do about it?

Now that I'm on the bus, some of my guilt and apprehension slips away. It's always like this. What's done is done. I settle back in my seat. Foolish woman. You'd think you were on your way to Australia for a year, not to the west coast for a few days.

"Why didn't you wait until next week, when I could come, too?" Mark asked me last night. Then he said, "Oh, I forgot, that's the whole idea, isn't it? To get away from me."

Oh Mark, my darling Mark. Do I really want to get away from you? You who I'd walk a mile out of my way on the chance of meeting when I was a girl. When I was seventeen I wrote in my diary, "If Mark loved me as I adore him I would be perfectly happy." Perfectly happy. Even the words sound antiquated.

No, it's not Mark I want to get away from so much as a condition, the condition of wife and mother and worrier. To be alone.

"I've never been alone." I tried to explain that to him last night. "Never in my whole life have I stayed in a hotel alone."

"Neither have I," he said, and I was surprised to realize this was true. But men don't seem to want to. They might crave other company, excitement, change. But not to be alone. We've had it all wrong for years, this man and woman business. The trapped man syndrome. The men I know don't seem to feel trapped at all. Ah, but their wives do.

For some reason I'm not very curious about the other people on the bus today. The man behind me sounds crabby and so does his wife. They're older than I am, in their late fifties, perhaps. They don't have much to talk about. Mark and I now, if we were on the bus together, we'd still have plenty to say to each other. It cheers me up a little to realize that. Years ago my mother, listening for our footsteps on the verandah steps late at night, would say, "Do you and Mark ever stop talking?" And sometimes, as she heard him begin to whistle the instant we said good-night, she'd say, "He must be glad to get away from you, girl." But we both knew it wasn't that.

I listen to some of the sparse conversation of the people behind me, and I hear her say to him: "If people hate each other, it's just as well." I wonder who, or what, they're talking about.

When the bus starts I have a moment of panic. The windows are wide, panoramic, and the sensation that the buildings we pass are themselves moving makes me feel dizzy and strange. I sometimes used to feel like that on the train when I was a child. I thought I'd be safe on a bus. I'm afraid of flying, though I do it at times, and I hate cars, especially on the highway. I hardly ever drive myself anymore. I wish I had brought some Valium with me, but I haven't taken anything like that for months. I'm neurotic, I suppose, but at least I'm used to it. I like Patsy Harvey's definition of neurotic. "More aware," she says, and, besides being complimentary, that fits the feeling better than anything a doctor or a psychiatrist has ever told me. I think of the skin on a newborn baby's head, not quite finished, where you can feel that vulnerable hollow, and see the pulse beat. I'm sure I've got a spot like that on my psyche. Nish, my mother used to call a sensitive or sore spot.

I read, and doze, and doze, and read, and then it's time for lunch. Still I'm alone, and it's still the way I want to be. Late in the afternoon a group of men get on, coastal boat employees going to join their ship. One man sits down beside me. There aren't many seats to spare. He seems tired, and at first we don't say anything. I look out the window, and he looks straight ahead. Then something sets us off, probably a question from me, and we chat intermittently for awhile. He begins to nod, and I decide I might as well have another nap, too. I can't get too much sleep these days. I don't fall off completely this time, but it interests me the way my body stays stiff and unyielding, as if I'm afraid that this man will get too close, that his head will drop to my shoulder, or mine to his. I'm not attracted to him, nor he to me, most likely, but it seems so stupid for both of us to be determined not to touch. Wouldn't it just be a nice friendly gesture if he could lay his head on my shoulder? I remember the times I've been lying on the chesterfield and Nigel, sitting on the floor, has let his head drop against my legs. He doesn't do that anymore. It's not the thing for a boy his age.

Thinking of the man next to me reminds me of the last time I was away without the family. That was for a conference, some kind of social action thing. I shared a room with another woman that time and with something going on every minute I hardly had time to realize I was away on my own. Except the night of the dance. That was different altogether.

I wasn't even going to go at first. It was about twenty years since I'd danced, and even when I was a young girl I wasn't very good at it. I don't like not being good at things, and I'm inclined to pretend I'm not interested in something when the plain truth is that I have no talent for it. Anyhow, I did go, persuading myself that it would be "snobbish" not to. There, now I can hear Beth again, saying, "Mom can forgive anyone anything just as long as they don't put on airs." God, they've got me so categorized I don't know where I leave off and they begin. I had a good time at the party, even got out and danced a couple of times. I didn't drink, of course. I never do.

After the dance, some of the others persuaded me to go back to the "hospitality suite." It was already two a.m. I don't know why I went. Yes, I do know. I went because I wanted to go. When I got there everybody was drinking and telling dirty jokes. Not everyone, but most. And some of them were really dirty, not funny-dirty like the ones Mark and I tell each other when we're alone. Or used to.

What am I doing here, I asked myself, especially after Tom sat down next to me. Tom was nice, and very attractive, in a lean, agile way. I knew he had spent the previous night with one of the women at the conference, Marie. I looked around for Marie, but she wasn't there.

Nobody seemed to know where she was, and most were too drunk to care.

Tom wasn't drunk, though, or at least not obviously. I wondered about him and Marie. So this was what went on at conferences, real cliché stuff. Had something gone wrong between them? They hadn't even met until the day before. Tom looked contented enough now. I wondered what I'd do if he put his arms around me. Almost everybody else in the room had paired off. The lights were still shining brightly, there was a lot of drinking going on, but couples were embracing all around us. Tom sat very close to me, but made no attempt to do anything else.

I looked across the room at Larry, a man I'd known for years. He had made a fumbling pass at me the night before, and I'd found this very hard to believe. I had never thought he was that kind of man. And where in the name of heaven had he got the idea I was that kind of woman? What kind of man? What kind of woman? Were there really different kinds? I had finally made Larry understand that I wasn't interested. It did my funny bone more good than my ego when I realized later that he had tried the same tactics with at least four other women besides myself. Finally, tonight, he had found someone: a dark-haired, pretty, older woman, who had seemed very quiet and withdrawn until now. Older woman. I was an older woman myself. About ten years older than Larry, and more than that older than Tom.

The jokes were getting dirtier. I didn't even try to laugh anymore. What would Mark say if he knew I was here? What would the children say? Probably have me all figured out, the way they always do. But no, I don't really think they'd like this.

Tom was telling a joke now, just to me. It was not repulsively vulgar, just funny, and I laughed. Of course I probably was just reacting to Tom the way he wanted me to react. I thought suddenly of the parties I used to go to when I was fourteen, fifteen. I had acted exactly the same way that I was acting tonight. A woman's libber, was I? A feminist, as I claimed? What a laugh. I was interested in Tom. I wanted him to be interested in me. What would I do if he was? What would I do if he wasn't? If Tom had been the one to make a pass at me, instead of Larry, would I have been so definite in my refusal? Did the whole thing just come down to physical attraction, after all? A magazine story I'd read several months before popped into my mind. It was written by a woman journalist who had gone to Nevada, where prostitution is legal, to do a story on a brothel there. She had been appalled at the careless ease with which the youngest prostitute, a beautiful girl just out of her teens, had snuggled up to her customer, a fat, beefy, middle-aged man who was rough and graceless in his approach. If only he were more attractive, the journalist kept thinking, I could understand it. Perhaps I'd even be tempted myself. And then she realized that she was well into the North American trap of physical attraction conquering, or excusing, all.

Tom and I sat there for about two hours. We talked, and laughed, and sometimes fell silent. Our hands weren't even touching. Meanwhile, the other couples were moving closer and closer to one another. Some had left the room. They were all married to other people. Just as Tom and I were.

If I just shifted my weight a little, I thought. Just leaned against him, ever so slightly. I wanted to, but I couldn't. And we kept on talking, and laughing, and sitting there.

I remembered the New Testament story about Jesus's condemnation of not just adultery but the unexpressed wish to commit adultery. I had always thought that pretty stern of Jesus, who was usually so gentle and understanding. Shouldn't we be given some credit for stifling our urges to stray? Were the urges themselves the sins? If it was a sin to be tempted, I was being sinful tonight.

Tom was looking at the woman who was singing. She really was an older woman, in her sixties at least, and her flat, monotonous voice was dragging out a ballad of the sea. She was sitting alone, very decorously, in the middle of an armchair. What did she think of the goings-on, I wondered? Evidently all this stopped at a certain age.

Adultery is for adults. I've heard that said jokingly more than once. Yes, and it seemed for youngish adults, at that. Most of the really older people at the conference had gone sensibly off to bed. I didn't see how that elderly singer had ended up here in the hospitality suite.

My daughters would think all those people crazy. In spite of all the talk about the new morality they are extremely moral about things like this. They might not think it necessary for two people to be married in order to live together, but they would feel that some kind of commitment is necessary, even if temporary. I have never heard either of them tell a dirty joke.

Tom had told me a lot about himself by now. People usually did that to me. He seemed to have had a hard life, especially when he was growing up. As a matter of fact, most of the people at the conference had been through experiences such as I had only read about. It was that kind of conference.

I looked at my watch. Four o'clock. The couples who were still in the room seemed to have settled down for the night. I moved a little away from Tom.

"I have to go now," I said. "My bedtime is long overdue." God, was that really me, saying something so sprightly and corny?

"Aw, do you have to?" he said. "Got to get your beauty sleep, I suppose." He made no move to come with me. "See you tomorrow," he said. I walked quickly across the room, out the door, and down the stairs to my own room. Alone.

Once there, away from the heated atmosphere of the hospitality suite, I felt strangely relieved. I took my time about going to bed, read the paper I'd bought earlier, and then lay awake for a long time in the dark. My roommate was not in her bed. I had not seen her since the dance. After all, I was glad to be sleeping alone. When I was almost asleep a startling thought pushed me awake. What if I had slept with someone, and picked up VD? I am, after all, allergic to penicillin. I giggled a little, and went to sleep. No pregnancy to worry about anymore, but there was always something for people like me.

In the morning I had breakfast with Marie. "Who did you pair off with last night?" she asked. She was obviously worried about Tom.

"No one," I said. "I don't do that." Then I smiled, to take the priggishness out of the words. "Besides, no one asked me."

Some people feel that what's all right for them is wrong for other people. I'm just the opposite. What's okay for Marie is not okay for me. There was a time when I would have disapproved of what she did; not anymore. But oh no, it wasn't for me. What kind of snobbishness is this? Beth would probably have the answer.

The conference ended that morning. I saw Tom once more. As I was leaving the hotel he and his friend Jack came up to me. We shook hands all round and Jack said, "We wanted to tell you what an impression you made on all of us, especially on Tommy and me." I felt a bit silly. "See you in town some time," Tom said. I just said, "So long, now."

They thought they were paying me a compliment but I wasn't sure. I felt like the schoolgirl who's always seen as a big sister. Still, they meant well. Neither of them would ever have said such a thing to Marie. I felt sorry for her, and envied her at the same time.

I went back on the bus that night, the same kind of bus I'm on now. That time, too, I sat next to a seaman who was going to the city to join his ship. Sailors must use the buses a lot. We talked a little, and then I leaned back and closed my eyes. After all, it had been about five that morning when I went to sleep. He started to sing. I held myself stiff and straight, just like this time, and that made it hard for me to drop off. I felt like giggling again. He went from "Me and Bobby McGee" to "Help me make it through the night" to "All I have to offer you is me." His voice was tuneful but he kept it low. Was I just imagining that his songs had meaning for me? Was I turning into one of those dreadful older women who imagines everyone is in love with her? He probably regarded me as the motherly type. Most people do. Still, the theme of his songs was remarkably consistent. Maybe that was just the kind he liked.

When I got home I told the family about Larry's funny-pathetic advances. That was safe enough; they all knew what Larry looked like. I told them carefully about the pairing off, even that I had been in the hospitality suite. They laughed with me. They trusted me. Why shouldn't they? I hadn't done anything wrong, had I?

Mark and I slept together that night. We sleep together every night, of course, but this was a bit different. I was glad to be home safe. Safe. Of course, if anything had happened with Tom it wouldn't have affected my feeling for Mark. Would it?

And now I'm going away again. We'll be there soon. I start to gather up my things, check my purse, reach for my coat. The man who was sitting beside me has moved to a seat with one of his friends. At least he didn't sing. He was nice, actually, a family man from one of the islands off the south coast. Someone else I'll never meet again.

I get off the bus and hail a taxi. The taximan talks a lot, and I don't have to say anything. He doesn't appear to see anything strange in a woman travelling alone. When I check in at the hotel I soon notice that there is no other woman there on her own. The guests are, overwhelmingly, male. A few are accompanied by their wives. I recognize a boy I went to school with, but he's checking out.

I sign the register and go to my room. It's a nice room, anonymous but comfortable. I think of the children and Mark at home, trying in their own way to get supper. I love them all. They're good to me, all of them. Perhaps they understand me better than I understand myself. Maybe, soon, I'll give up all this nonsense and stay home like the sensible, middle-aged woman I'm supposed to be. Meanwhile, I go to the bathroom to get ready for dinner. It will be good to sit at a table and eat a meal I haven't cooked, not worry about whose turn it is to do the dishes and end up doing them myself, not have to think about what time Nigel comes in tonight, or what he's doing, or with whom. Everything, for the moment, is beautifully out of my hands.

Moving Day

I suppose it shouldn't have come as such a shock to me really. I mean, all I heard at the university for the whole year was centralization, resettlement, relocation—the professors had a real field day, especially the ones in the Sociology Department. And the newspapers, too, it was a godsend for them. As for the politicians—well. In fact the only people who haven't had too much to say about it are the ones who are really involved in the thing. But anyway, as I said, I shouldn't have been so surprised when I heard that everybody from Grassy Island was going to move to Carlisle. It was Karen who brought it up.

"But why didn't Mom and Dad tell me?" I was talking to myself although Karen was sitting right next to me on the train.

"They probably wanted to surprise you with the good news when you got home." Karen is from Carlisle herself and of course she thinks there's no place like it.

"I can think of more pleasant surprises," I told her, and then I changed the subject. Somehow I didn't want to discuss it with Karen.

When I got home, though, I lost no time in bringing up the matter, I can tell you. They were all on the wharf to meet the boat, all except Mom and Nan, that is. It took the two of them to look after the big Welcome Home Dinner. I couldn't get a word in edgeways going up the hill, what with Cavell and Charlie asking a thousand questions. Dad didn't say much. He never does.

But when we were all sitting around the table, after Mom had hugged me and Nan had cried her little cry, I let go.

"What's all this I hear about leaving Grassy Island, Mom?" It was a long time since I'd had chicken and salt meat on the same plate but I wasn't as hungry as I'd expected to be. "It's not true, I hope."

You know how they always used to say in old-fashioned books, "Her face fell"? Well, that's what happened to Mom's face then. "Yes, it is true, Jenny," she said slowly. "I thought you'd be glad."

Well after that everyone got into the act—Nan telling Mom that "everybody is not in such a rush to get away as you is, Martha," and Cavell and Charlie both saying they didn't know what anyone could see in a place like Carlisle. Even Dad had his say. "It's the women that's doing it," he told me. "If it was left to us men we'd all be content to live out our lives here."

And didn't Mom go for him when he said that—all about the men being away in the lumber woods or on the Labrador when things were really rough on the Island, and how she was sick and tired of not being able to get a doctor when she needed one, and of having her children go to a one-room school under teachers too young or too stupid to get a job anywhere else. Then when Nan said she didn't see how Mom could go away and leave the place where dear little Tommy was buried—well, that was too much even for Mom. Tommy was my little brother, died when he was three years old, pneumonia, I think it was. But Dad took up for Mom then and reminded Nan that if she was the good Christian woman she was supposed to be she'd know it wouldn't matter where the poor little body lay. The next thing I knew I was up in my room bawling my eyes out. It wasn't a bit like the kind of homecoming I'd been looking forward to for months.

I suppose I must have fallen asleep, for the next thing I knew the house was quiet and Mom was standing in the doorway just looking at me. When she saw that I was awake she came in and sat on the bed, not even pushing back the spotless white spread she always ironed so carefully.

"Try to see it my way, Jenny," she pleaded, and it did seem strange to hear Mom plead. She's usually so sure of herself.

"I'm sorry, Mom. I shouldn't have been so upset, but I can't imagine any home except this one, and I don't know how I can live if I don't have this place to come back to."

"To come back to. That's just the point, Jenny." Mom stood up then, and walked over to the window. I couldn't see her face. "I wouldn't mind coming back here for the rest of my life. But it's *living* here, day in, day out, season in, season out, year in, year out, that I can't take any longer. It was bad enough when there were twenty or more families here, but now there's only eight left, and more going all the time. Things'll get worse instead of better." She ran her hand along the shiny-painted windowsill. "If you had to settle down here yourself, Jenny, you'd know what I mean."

She did have something there, though I wasn't willing to concede it then. I had never considered settling down on Grassy Island myself, but I'm going to be a teacher, after all, so I'll *have* to go away. And then, when I do marry Ralph, he'll probably still be working in Corner Brook, where he is now, so I'll have to live there. But I had always counted on Grassy Island as being *there* when I needed it. I would never be able to feel the same way about Carlisle.

Well, somehow things got back to normal after that first awful day. It was as if we had all made up our minds, on our own, not to bring the matter up. Everything was finalized, anyhow, so what was the use? Evidently Mom had been one of the instigators of the whole project and this was what was annoying Nan. But Nan didn't have much left to say, except a scattered word under her breath and Mom ignored that.

We had a wonderful summer. Even the weather cooperated, for once, and we spent more time outdoors than in. Between the boats and the berries, the grass and the gardens, we didn't have an idle minute. It was like we couldn't get enough of it all. But you know, even though Mom didn't say another word to me about moving, except what she had to in the way of preparation, sometimes I couldn't help seeing her side of it. I still couldn't picture myself in Carlisle, but after all, I wouldn't be there very much, and it *would* be better for Mom. I had never really realized before how much she must have hated the isolation of the island all those years. It would probably turn out to be good for Cavell and Charlie, too. As for Dad, well, he seemed closer to being reconciled than he had been at first. One night I even caught him looking at the pictures of modern kitchens in Eaton's catalogue. He always did like carpentry work next best to fishing.

Mom was quieter than I ever remembered her. Sometimes I'd catch her looking at me, as if she was about to say something, and then she'd change her mind. She had a lot of work to do, of course, and although Cavell and I helped she had her own way of doing things and didn't want to be interfered with too much. One night, when she was taking a batch of bread out of the oven in the old wood stove, Dad laughed and said to her, "I suppose the bread'll taste better when we gets electricity, Martha," and she snapped right back, "Are you trying to tell me I don't make good bread, Peter Mead?" But most of the time she was unusually silent. I figured it was because she had her sights set on Carlisle and was almost afraid to breathe for fear something would go wrong with the plan.

But nothing did, and almost before we could turn around it was moving day. We were all standing on the wharf watching Dad load our gear aboard Uncle Job's boat. Some of it had gone on ahead of us, but there were certain things that we couldn't take until the last day.

Cavell and Charlie were horsing around threatening to throw each other overboard, and Nan was sitting on an overturned barrel, her ankles tightly crossed, looking almost as if she was enjoying the excitement.

"Where's your mother?" she asked suddenly. "I thought by the way she been dyin' to get out of here that she'd be the first one on board."

"She must have gone back to the house for something. Run up and get her, Jenny, we're almost ready," Dad said, and I went to find her.

Mom was just standing in the middle of the kitchen when I got there and I had the "Hurry up" formed on my lips before I got a good look at her. Even though her back was towards me the sight of her shoulders was enough to make me swallow the words I was about to say. Quiet though she was, I knew that she was sobbing her heart out.

I slipped out of the house and hurried back to the wharf. I felt I shouldn't hang around. "Mom'll be down in a minute," I told Dad. "She's just...having a last look."

I wondered if I should tell him more but just at that moment his eyes met mine and I could see there was no need. "I'll go and get her myself, Jenny maid," he said, and our eyes followed him as he ran up the path. Even Nan didn't have a word to say.

A Different Person

Susan parked the car carefully and prayed a silent prayer that it would still be there when she got back. Who was it had told her about cars being stolen from airport parking lots? She couldn't remember, and it didn't matter anyway. Did her car insurance cover theft? She was never really certain about things like that.

She took her new leather suitcase from the trunk and considered whether to carry it or pull it along casually, the way flight attendants did. Little things like that always worried her. Had she left anything behind? She never did leave anything behind, but she always checked, just to make sure.

She was far too early, as usual. Now she'd have to wait over an hour in the terminal before her flight was called. She envied people who arrived at the last minute, rushed through baggage check and security and climbed aboard the plane breathless and smiling. She knew she could never do that.

It was a lovely morning. There'd be no takeoff problems. The sky was beautifully clear, promising another perfect day. Good flying weather. Whenever she thought about it she was always surprised that she wasn't afraid of flying. Lucky she wasn't, in this job.

After she had checked her suitcase she went to the little bookstore next to the restaurant. When she travelled she always brought along something by Jane Austen or George Orwell or Virginia Woolf but she usually ended up reading a Sidney Sheldon or a Judith Krantz. There was something about flying that called for trash.

She looked at the books on display. Lots of Harlequins, but even on a plane she could never get interested in those. A funny-looking thing called *Single Lady*, the cover showing a wild-haired female with five men apparently growing out of her hair.

Ah, this next one looked promising. *Why Marry?* it was called. It was by a pair of psychologists, probably married to each other, whose faces beamed out from the back cover. The front cover showed an attractive young woman striding confidently along the street in that *Charlie* cologne advertisement style, head thrust back and long blond hair flowing out behind her. At the extreme left of the picture a young man was watching the young woman. She appeared not to know he was there.

She bought the book, along with the latest *People* magazine, and put them both into her large handbag. Next, a cup of tea and some toast. The toast was good here. She should know if anyone did. Since she had taken this new job setting up conferences she seemed to be spending more time at the airport than anywhere else. She enjoyed the job; when she was working she forgot everything else. She liked the sense of confidence, of self-assurance it gave her, which she rarely experienced at other times.

Deirdre, who'd had the job for two years before Susan took it over, gave it up when she got married. Susan suspected it was because Deirdre's husband didn't want her to be travelling all the time, but of course Deirdre would not admit that.

"I'm tired of it," she told Susan when she was helping her to get adjusted. "Two years on the road is a long time. Everything gets stale."

Deirdre's new job wasn't quite a promotion, more of a lateral transfer. Mostly public relations, not really very exciting. But Deirdre...Deirdre, of all people...was excited about her marriage and her new life with a man who'd been married before and had two small children.

"Ken's had a hard time," she said when she first told Susan about the wedding plans. "His wife just walked out one day and never came back. He doesn't even know where she is. I think it's greatly to his credit that he kept the children." Sometimes it occurred to Susan that Deirdre didn't sound like herself anymore. "He could easily have let his mother take them over." Susan had met them, a boy of nine and girl of seven. They were very quiet and well-behaved.

She liked Ken, and was glad for Deirdre. She hoped they'd continue to be happy. But Deirdre's plans had come as something of a shock, for she had always proclaimed, loudly and emphatically, that marriage was not for her. She'd always had plenty of men friends, a girl as attractive as Deirdre was bound to, but she had been so content in her small apartment, with its daring reds and greens, its huge cushions and its striped walls. Now she was living in Ken's house, surrounded by pastel walls and grey-blue carpets.

"The loneliness started to get to me," she told Susan. "It was fun at first, doing exactly what I wanted to do, having to answer to nobody, going and coming as I pleased. But the novelty wears off after awhile."

What about your marriage? Won't the novelty wear off that, too? Susan didn't say the words but that didn't stop her from thinking them.

She looked around the restaurant. It was beginning to fill up now. Next to her sat a smartly-dressed couple with two little girls, both holding well-dressed Cabbage Patch dolls. Probably going to Florida, though it was a bit late in the year for that. They were all eating, carefully and self-consciously. Another table was crowded with what looked like a large family. Only one of them, a large, middle-aged woman in a sky-blue pantsuit, appeared to be going away. The others had obviously come to see her off. They all looked close to tears. Susan tried to remember the last time anyone had seen her off.

"There's not one bit of need," she'd told her sister Marian. "It'll all be so commonplace after awhile, like going to work in an office. I don't want people getting up out of bed at ungodly hours to come to the airport with me."

As she moved toward the security area Susan passed close to a couple with their arms wrapped tightly around each other, their lips clinging together in a long, passionate kiss. She recognized the man; tall, skinny and wearing a large, flamboyant hat, he was involved with a local collective theatre group. The girl, small and fragile, with long, kinky blond hair, clung to him as if she would never let him go. Blinking, Susan turned and looked hard in the other direction. How long was it since she'd been kissed, really kissed, by a man? She had never been kissed like that.

On the plane Susan began to read the *People* magazine, not wanting her seat-mate, a silvery-haired businessman, to see the title of the paperback. There'd be plenty of time for that one later on, when she got to the hotel. The magazine had the usual mixture of stories about show business types, other celebrities and dedicated scientists. The cover story featured a couple, the woman vaguely familiar from a family television series, who were happy at last. When entertainers were written up by *People* they were always "happy at last." They might have a history of broken marriages, shattered love affairs, drug problems, nervous breakdowns, alcoholism, but they had all, finally, found true happiness. "After therapy, two divorces and the ups and downs of a show business career she feels good about life with Brant," burbled the text. Not all that different from the old fairy tales where Prince Charming came along and made everything right. In this case it was Prince Charming Number 3, but did that really matter? Not in *People* magazine, certainly.

God, I really am getting cynical, she thought, closing the magazine and putting it back in her handbag. I used to be able to lose myself in this kind of stuff.

The man next to her was reading some typed papers. She rarely did anything like that on a plane, but she had noticed several times before that men often did. He had probably got his secretary to prepare the material before he left. He shifted in his seat and his arm touched hers. The electric shock feeling ran through her again. When this kind of thing started happening, several years before, she had thought she must be some kind of sex maniac. She had grown used to it, could even laugh to herself about it, remembering confession stories she'd read in her early teens, smuggling them into the house so her mother wouldn't see them. Still, she often wondered if other women in real life experienced the same kind of thing, or if men did. She could never quite get the nerve to ask anyone, although she had come close once, with Deirdre. "If a woman was sitting in the dark and another woman touched her, she'd probably get exactly the same feeling as if it were a man," she'd heard Deirdre say. Susan wasn't sure if that was true or not. All she knew was that she herself never got the electric shock feeling when she brushed against a woman. She couldn't remember ever having brushed against anyone in the dark.

Sometimes Susan thought that things had been a lot simpler in her mother's day. Or even her sister Marian's. Marian, who was forty, had been married since she was twenty-one. "You don't know how lucky you are, Sue," she said, every time she came to Susan's apartment for a quiet cup of tea and a chance to put her feet up. "Marriage is not all it's cracked up to be. And children certainly aren't." Still, Marian seemed reasonably happy, most of the time. Her four children were growing up and she was beginning to have more time for herself. Her husband, too, was nice enough, quiet, perhaps a little too quiet, but there were worse faults. Marian and Bill had been going together since high school and had married as a matter of course, the way most other young couples had done then. By the time Susan was in her early twenties, everything was different.

For the first few years of her working life Susan had considered herself very lucky to be a young single woman in what was surely a heyday for young single women. Popular magazines and television shows portrayed single women as brave, full of life, warm, gutsy, funny (oh, how they loved that word) and sexy. Nobody expected you to get married as a matter of course anymore. Or, as her Uncle Philip, who considered himself a great wit was fond of saying, a matter of intercourse. Very few people asked, "Why isn't a nice girl like you married?" They might think it, but they didn't ask it, except perhaps for some elderly man or woman who didn't know about women's liberation. She was thirty-two now, and she was pretty sure no one had ever referred to her as an old maid.

But single bliss wasn't all it was cracked up to be, either. At least not for her. As she got older her dates, if they could still be called dates, got fewer and fewer. Were there really any single girls, or women, around like Mary Tyler Moore, queen of the reruns? On the show (and perhaps in real life too) everyone who met Mary appeared to fall in love with her, and she always knew how to handle every situation, though she made a great show of being confused. Deirdre had reminded Susan of Mary, for a few years. Susan dreaded going out with a new man. You'd think it would have gotten easier, after all this time. Instead it was getting harder.

Susan wasn't very active in the women's movement but she did go to meetings occasionally, especially when they dealt with pension rights, equal pay for work of equal value or the building of confidence. She had gone just twice to consciousness-raising sessions but even while they were going on she knew she wouldn't dare continue. Sooner or later she'd have to speak out for herself, and she was convinced she'd never be able to do that. It was embarrassing enough listening to the others. They talked about their sexual practices, what their husbands or mates expected of them and what they expected of their men. Some reached back into their childhood, telling of sexual experiences with older relatives, or even with their fathers. Nothing like that had ever happened to Susan. Her father, a painfully shy man, had always been kind and gentle toward her and toward everyone else but she had never felt that she knew him very well. Though her uncles had little to talk about when they ran out of jokes, there was nothing unpleasant about them. Sometimes, listening to the other women, she marvelled at how dull and safe her life had been. And still was.

Of course she could have told them about her fantasies. They were exciting enough. What would these women think if she started to pour out her imaginary passionate love affairs with the stranger on the train, the handsome young black boy at the beach, the man who sat next to her at dinner? In all of those fantasies she was the aggressor, the beautiful temptress no man could resist. Most of her lovers were dream figures, conjured up into an ongoing story in her mind. But sometimes they were real men, men she knew well or slightly, some married, some single, others little more than boys. Once, on a long train ride, she had made a list in her notebook of all the men she had been attracted to, then had tucked the notebook hastily into her bag, ashamed of her silliness. I've probably had more one-sided love affairs, with the other person knowing absolutely nothing about them, than any other woman on earth, she thought.

Susan smiled to herself, glad her seat companion could not read her mind. He had put away his reports now and was reading the *Financial Post*. Probably not a very interesting person. She was immediately conscious that he had very likely made the same assessment of her. She edged farther away from him so there'd be no further shocks.

Perhaps if she'd continued to go to the consciousness-raising sessions she'd at least have found out if the others got turned on as easily as she did. Sometimes she wondered if it was because she was so much alone, or would it still have happened if she had a husband and four kids, like Marian? For a person who indulged so little in any kind of sexual activity she appeared to be disproportionately aware of it.

You can always masturbate, was the cool advice of some feminist writers. She had even heard some of her women's movement friends say the same thing. "Sex with someone I love," Woody Allen called masturbation. But for her it was a poor substitute. How could you cuddle up to yourself? She stifled a giggle, again relieved that nobody could read her thoughts.

She recalled a novel she'd read about a female archaeologist who, especially when she was travelling, was attracted to almost every man she met. The big difference between her and Susan was that the archaeologist usually did something about it. She fell easily into bed with almost anyone, although she'd had one husband and still had a permanent lover. And yet she didn't come across as cheap or hard. Maybe that was because she was English, and highbrow English at that.

Susan knew several girls and women, right in her own town, who did the same thing. There was Cynthia, who'd been divorced when she was very young and whose affairs were the talk of the office building. There was Gail, still not as old as Susan, who had already lived with three different men. Serial monogamy, she called it. And there was Vera, married with three children, who routinely picked up men and discarded them just as quickly.

Most of her single friends weren't like that at all. They went to "respectable" bars in groups of three or four, and went home the same way. They took trips to the Caribbean or Hawaii or Mexico, usually still in groups of three or four. They looked good, dressed well, kept their figures and held their own in conversation. Susan didn't know how any of them felt about men, or sex, or themselves.

The women she had met at the feminist meeting seemed more open. But most of them were married, or had been married, or were living with someone. Not many of them were like herself.

Like herself. What was that like? If she didn't know herself, how could she expect anyone else to understand her? She had never made a conscious decision to stay single. It had just happened. Her life, for the most part, was pretty good. She liked her job, she had many friends (not intimate friends, but you can't have everything), a nice apartment, a devoted family nearby and nieces and nephews who gave her great pleasure. Sometimes Amy, her youngest niece, came to stay with her on weekends. "Why isn't there a daddy here, Aunt Susie?" she had asked the first time, looking around as if to see one emerge from hiding. "Because I'm not married, Amy." "Does that mean you can't have babies, then?" "Yes, Amy, I guess it does mean that." "That's okay, Aunt Susie, you can have me whenever you want me." "The best of all possible worlds," Marian had said when Susan told her.

Why does it all have to bother me so much? Susan glanced quickly at her seat-mate, who had discarded the *Financial Post* and was now reading *Time* magazine. At least he was an improvement on the man who'd sat next to her last time. He had spilled his drink all over her skirt. Why can't I be like Aunt May? She just goes to her job and to her card club and for drives in the country with friends. She travels to all those out-of-the-way places nobody else ever thinks of going to. She's fat and her hair is grey and she laughs a lot and people really like her. I'm sure she never thinks about men the way I do. Was she always like that, or did she just get that way at a certain age?

Susan looked at her watch. They'd be landing in about half an hour. She took out her little brown notebook and studied the name of the man who'd be meeting her at the airport. Arthur Adams. A nice name, alliterative even. He was a university extension worker, fairly new at his job, and he had never set up a conference before. She would have plenty of work to do, at least until the sessions were all underway.

She thought again of the last conference she had helped arrange. It was in a small town, much smaller than the one she was going to now. She had worked on it with a man named Ronald Mathieson. It was very late, the night before the conference, when they had finally finished preparing all the kits and getting everything ready for the opening the next morning. He had suggested going to a little restaurant nearby for a cup of tea, since everything in the hotel was closed up.

A cup of tea. Most men suggested a drink. Susan had often wished she could allow herself to drink more. Perhaps she'd loosen up then, let herself go the way she wanted to. But every time she tried to talk herself into taking more than two drinks the fear of making a fool of herself overcame everything else. She usually drank white wine or vodka and tonic, with lots of tonic. On special occasions she'd splurge with a Singapore Sling.

She and Ronald were the only two customers in the tiny restaurant. He looked tired. His light brown hair, carefully combed back at the beginning of the evening, was falling over his forehead. His shirt was rumpled, the top button undone. She felt a rush of tenderness for him.

He talked to her about his wife Margaret, their children, the extension they were building on their house. She told him about her parents, the job, Marian and the children, Deirdre's marriage. She found him extraordinarily easy to talk to. He seemed to find her the same way.

Susan couldn't believe it was herself talking when she suggested they play something on the big old jukebox in the corner. She pressed the keys for Willie Nelson's *Blue Eyes Cryin' in the Rain* and he chose Dan Hill with *Sometimes When We Touch*. There were very few current numbers listed. We're like two teenagers, she thought, remembering those earlier jukebox days when nothing in the world mattered except the boy sitting beside you. She was glad her feminist friends couldn't see her now.

For one wild, idiotic moment she thought of asking him to dance. She was a good dancer; he looked as if he might be too. It would be like something out of one of her fantasies, holding him close and moving slowly around with him in the small space between the booths. Of course she didn't ask him. It probably didn't occur to him to ask her.

In her fantasies she always wore something revealing. Her figure was fuller, lusher, than it actually was. In real life the clothes she allowed herself were more conservative. That night she had been wearing a soft, cream-coloured blouse with a bow, and a dark brown suit. She had taken off the jacket when they sat down.

They stayed in the restaurant for a long time, listening to the music and sipping tea. He had already told her he was staying at the hotel for the conference because his home was too far out of town to commute easily.

"I guess we'd better go." They both said it together, and then they both laughed. He took her arm to guide her to the car. It was a very dark night.

When they reached her room he unlocked the door for her, stepped inside and turned on the light. "Well, goodnight, now," he said. "I'll see you in the morning." He held out his hand.

After he was gone she lay awake for an hour, remembering all the small, inconsequential things they had said to each other. Why hadn't she stepped forward when he held out his hand? Why hadn't she touched him, put her hands on his shoulders, let him know what she wanted him to do? The desk clerk had seen them come in together. He had probably drawn his own conclusions already, if he was not too bored to notice such things.

Afterwards, she persuaded herself to be glad she had made no move. She probably would have frightened poor Ronald to death. During the conference itself she saw little of him, except when there were other people around. At the closing banquet she met his wife, a fair-haired, fragile-looking woman who talked about their children.

Now, on the plane, the flight attendant was checking to see that all the seats were upright. Susan buckled her seatbelt. The man beside her put his papers and magazines into his briefcase and sat back, waiting. They had not exchanged one word.

"You must have a ball in that job," her friend Zita, who worked for the telephone company, had said to her. "I suppose you're a different person when you're away from home."

"You'd be surprised," said Susan, rolling her eyes and wiggling her hips.

A different person. She thought about the words as she held herself tightly against the seat-back, waiting for the plane's first contact with the ground. She looked out through the window; the weather was still fine and sunny. Somewhere inside the terminal building Arthur Adams would be waiting for her. Whoever he was.

Mainly Because of the Meat

"What's the matter with you, Debbie? You look like you're somewhere else. Anything wrong?"

"Oh, hi, Phyllis. I didn't even see you there. Am I in your way? Hurry up and punch, now. You've only got half a minute."

Debbie stood back while Phyllis put her punch card through the machine. Then they walked together to adjoining check-out counters.

"You didn't answer me, Deb. Is anything wrong?"

"Nothing more than usual. I was just kind of in a daze, listening to what everyone was saying without really taking it in. It takes me a while Monday mornings to get adjusted to this place."

"Same here. Did you have a nice weekend?"

"All right, I guess. Saturday night we went to the Steamer but my feet were so tired I spent most of the night sitting down. Rob didn't like that too well. What about yourself?"

"I was in the house the whole time. No, that's a lie, we did drop up to Mom's yesterday evening. She's not very well lately. But Saturday night we didn't have a babysitter, and no money to pay for one, really, so myself and Dave just sat home and watched T.V. We ordered a pizza, so it wasn't too bad. He was just as tired as I was."

"Yeah, some life, hey? Do you ever wonder what we're all workin' for? The money goes out faster than it comes in, right? And it must be worse for you, trying to save up for a house and everything."

"You should be doin' the same thing. You and Rob are goin' out a long time now, aren't you?"

"I don't know if I ever want to get married. Seems like it only makes everything harder. I looks at Mom and Dad sometimes and I can't help wondering what in the world they're gettin' out of it all. Still four more youngsters to put through school and as soon as that's over it'll be almost time for Dad to be pensioned. Then I s'pose one of 'em'll get sick, like so many more do."

"Well, you don't needto have a big family. Thank God for the pill. But are you sure there's nothing else wrong? I can usually depend on you to get me up out of the dumps."

"I don't know, girl. It's just that things get too much for me sometimes. Down to the Steamer the other night I was lookin' at the university crowd. You can tell 'em just by lookin' at 'em. For one thing, they don't dress up like we do. But they're the ones got an easy life ahead of 'em. They'll be doctors or lawyers or...."

"Or Indian chiefs. I know what you mean. Some of them got it hard too, though. They're not all rich."

Debbie went to the safe for her cash-tray and put it into the register. Already there were customers in the supermarket and she didn't even have her counter scrubbed down yet. Where in the world did they all come from so early on a Monday morning? That girl with the baby, she came in almost every day. The baby was laughing out loud as his mother spun him around and around in the cart.

"Want to use my pail of water for your counter, Debbie?" Phyllis called out. "It's still hot."

"Heavens, are you finished already? Okay, thanks. I'm slow this morning."

"Good morning, Debbie." Mr. Marshall was standing beside the check-out.

"Good morning, Mr. Marshall." She kept on scrubbing the conveyor belt. It was a hard thing to get clean.

"Everything all right?"

"Yes, I think so, Mr. Marshall."

"You're a good worker, Debbie, a good, fast worker. That's why it surprises me when I have a complaint about you."

Debbie looked up at him and said nothing.

"Mrs. Allen phoned me Saturday night after I got home. You know Mrs. Allen, don't you?"

Debbie knew Mrs. Allen very well. She had gone to school with Mrs. Allen's daughter, Christina. Christina had the kind of bedroom that Debbie used to think belonged only to girls in the old television shows like *Happy Days* and *Who's the Boss*. They had been good friends.

"Yes, I know her. I served her Saturday, almost closing time it was." She remembered Mrs. Allen's groceries: T-Bone steaks, a Tendersweet ham, table butter, fancy cheese and fresh pineapple. And lots of other things.

"Mrs. Allen told me she was missing two bags of groceries. She said she checked very carefully when she got home and she was short several items. I believe you packed her groceries yourself."

"That's right. I did. Tommy was...he was busy doing something else."

"Mrs. Allen will be in shortly to replace the missing items. She said she didn't want to get you into trouble but she had to be specific. I told her you'd just put it through on a No Charge. Of course this means someone ended up with two extra bags of stuff and for sure they'll never report it. You'll have to be more careful, Debbie. The store can't afford to lose money like that. And Mrs. Allen is one of our best customers."

Debbie held her lips tightly together as Mr. Marshall walked back towards the boys who were stocking the shelves. She was finding it harder and harder, lately, to keep from answering back. But she couldn't afford to lose her job, at least not until she finished her typing course. And if she didn't start getting more time to practise she would never finish it. She scrubbed fiercely at the ground-in dirt on the conveyor belt. When she looked up, Phyllis was waving at her from the next check-out. "The store can't afford to lose money," she mouthed, in perfect imitation of Mr. Marshall's lip formation. "Remember that now, Miss Evans." In spite of herself, Debbie laughed out loud.

"It's good to hear people laughing so early in the morning." The girl with the baby was standing at Debbie's check-out. She pushed two oranges and a can of Pepsi towards Debbie, and then pulled a two-dollar bill from her jacket pocket. The baby was eating a chocolate bar.

"My, Jason, you're getting yourself in some state." The girl bent over, moistened a tissue with her own saliva and began to wipe the baby's face. When he squirmed and started to whimper his mother hastily shoved the candy bar back in his mouth.

"Hi, Jason," said Debbie, smiling at him. He grinned back, his small mouth covered with sticky chocolate. "He's cute," she said, handing the girl her change. "How old is he?"

"Almost ten months. No, it's all gone, Jason." She took the wrapper from him and put it on the counter. "Don't cry now, you're not gettin' another one." She opened her purse and took out a ring with two keys on it, which she passed to the baby, who seemed to be considering whether or not it was worth his while to keep on crying. "They're sweet but they'd drive you foolish sometimes," she said to Debbie. "I been tryin' to get a job. Do they need anyone here?"

Debbie looked at the girl's slight frame, her pale skin and tired-looking eyes. "You could fill out an application form. Get one from the office. What grade have you got?"

"Well, I finished Grade Ten. I started Grade Eleven, but then...." She shrugged her shoulders, and nodded towards the baby. "I don't know who I'd get to look after him, though. Mom says she's not going to start all over again with someone else's youngsters." She picked up the baby and her parcel, pushed the cart away and started toward the office.

"Good morning, Debbie." Mrs. Allen must have just come in. No Monday morning disarray for her. Every carefully-coloured hair was in place; her face looked like an advertisement for 2nd Debut.

"Did Mr. Marshall tell you about my problem?" She smiled widely, and Debbie thought of her own mother who rarely opened her mouth when she smiled because of the two teeth missing from her plate. She had broken them off years before and was forever planning to go to the denturist for a new set.

"I hope I didn't get you into trouble, dear, but of course I had to call Mr. Marshall when I realized what had happened. None of us can afford to lose money today, can we? You do understand?"

Debbie's own smile was stiff. "Yes, of course, Mrs. Allen. Just go ahead and pick up what you're missing."

"How is your mother, Debbie?" Mrs. Allen seemed determined to be even friendlier than usual. "I haven't seen her at church for several weeks."

"Oh, Mom's all right." Debbie certainly wasn't going to tell Mrs. Allen that her mother had vowed, swearing vehemently, not to set foot inside the church again until she got a new coat. "She's a bit tired on Sundays, usually."

"Oh, I know she has a lot to do, and I think she's wonderful, bringing up such a large family without...." Her voice trailed off but Debbie knew what she'd been going to say. "I know you're a great help to her, dear," Mrs. Allen continued, putting her hand on Debbie's arm. "But I hope you're not going to stay here forever. This is just a stopgap for you, isn't it? You always were such a bright child at school."

Debbie said nothing.

"Christina was asking about you in her last letter. She's having a wonderful time in Toronto. I just couldn't stand the idea of sending her to university here. You know what a dive it is, full of drug pushers and other strange types." She paused and then went on. "Tina said she'd been to some sort of lecture on that woman who wrote the *Anne of Green Gables* books. What was her name?"

"L.M. Montgomery." Debbie's legs felt as if they weren't there.

"Yes, that's the one. I know the two of you used to get all her books out of the library when you were going to school. You were always talking about going to Prince Edward Island. Tina said she was sorry you weren't there to hear the lecture too."

Debbie felt herself a relax a little. Yes, Christina really would be sorry about that. Sometimes Debbie forgot what a nice girl Tina was.

"My, Tina must have enjoyed that. We really loved those Anne books when we were in Grade Seven and Eight.

"Well, dear, I guess I'd better go and pick up my things. Tell your mother I was asking about her. We're having a sale of work and afternoon tea at the church next week. I hope she'll be able to come along." She pulled out a shopping cart and walked toward the fruit section.

"Hey, Miss?"

Debbie turned around to find a short, fat woman, a customer she'd often served before, standing at the check-out. She had nothing in her hands except a shiny black plastic purse out of which she was taking a cigarette. She lit the cigarette, inhaled deeply, and then looked sideways at Debbie.

"What can I do for you, ma'am?"

"Well, it's like this, see. When I got home Sat'day night I couldn't find half the stuff I bought. Someone else must of took some of my groceries by mistake. Can I pick up what's missing, like that other woman is doing?"

She wet her finger and began to rub at a spot on her red crimpknit slacks.

Debbie hesitated for a moment.

"Did I serve you?"

The woman shifted from one foot to the other. She kept on rubbing at the spot as she spoke.

"To tell you the truth, girl, I can't remember. You often do serve me, but Sat'day night I had that much on my mind I can hardly remember anything."

Debbie couldn't remember either. It had been a very busy evening and sometimes, when she was extra tired, she didn't even look at the faces of the people she was checking through.

"You better go and ask Mr. Marshall, anyhow. I don't see why he wouldn't let you pick up what you didn't get. You know which one he is, do you?"

"That's the boss, is it? Dark-haired fella with the big nose? Okay, I'll ask him."

"Better watch that one, Deb." Phyllis had left her own check-out and was leaning over Debbie's, watching the woman walk toward where Mr. Marshall was standing, "She's a hard case."

"What do you mean?"

"Always tryin to get something for nothing. She was all ears when you were talking to Mrs. Allen. You've seen her in here with that crowd of youngsters, haven't you?"

Of course. Debbie remembered the children now. About five of them there were, noisy and not very clean.

"Yeah, I've seen her. She looks too old to have youngsters that small though, don't she?"

"I believe they're her grandchildren. Something happened to the daughter. I don't know if she got sick now, or took off, or what."

"Excuse me, miss." Debbie turned to find an irritated looking old man at the check-out. "Do you *work* here or are you paid to chat with the other employees?"

The time passed quickly. It was amazingly busy for a Monday morning. Mrs. Allen came back, checked through her cottage cheese, her bananas, her avocados, her cauliflower, her frozen strawberries, her back bacon and her ground steak.

"Everything all right, Mrs. Allen?" Mr. Marshall was forever appearing from nowhere.

"Oh, just fine, thanks, Mr. Marshall. I've got to hurry home now before my cold things get warm."

Debbie packed the groceries with a solicitude that was mostly forced. Mr. Marshall was, after all, watching her every move. And she had nothing against Mrs. Allen, really.

"Thank you very much, Debbie dear. Remember to tell your mother what I said, now. And don't forget to drop Christina a line. She doesn't want to lose touch with her old friends."

The next few minutes were slack enough for Debbie to watch through the big window until Mrs. Allen, after carefully arranging her packages in the back seat, got into her shining dark-green Chrysler and drove slowly away. She thought of Tina in her third year at the University in Toronto. Just like the girls they used to read about in *Seventeen* and *Flare*. Debbie had never in her whole life read a story about a girl who worked in a supermarket.

She turned her head to find Mr. Marshall staring at her from the little window in the office. "Even if you're not busy, *look* busy," she muttered to herself. She moved the magazines around in their racks, although they had not been disturbed yet this morning. When she straightened the candy display behind her check-out she realized that three of the chocolate bar six-packs had been "tampered with," as Mr. Marshall liked to put it. There was a Cherry Blossom missing from each. She smiled as she recalled a skit she'd once seen about an enormously fat shoplifter who was addicted to Cherry Blossom bars. Then she sighed. Mr. Marshall wouldn't have found that skit at all funny.

"Look at your friend," Phyllis called softly, pointing toward the woman in the red slacks who was wheeling a full cart toward Debbie's counter. "I've never seen her get that many groceries before."

Debbie hadn't either. Mrs. Molloy—that was her name, Molloy—rarely picked up more than eight or ten items at a time.

"Can you check me through now, Miss?" Mrs. Molloy sounded out of breath. Her face was red and shiny and her hands were shaking a little on the cart handle. She looks like she might have high blood pressure, Debbie thought.

"I'm in a bit of a rush," she said, pulling some vegetables out of her cart and putting them on the belt. "I got to take one of the youngsters down to the hospital as soon as my son gets back with the car. She've had an earache since Friday and she haven't stopped screechin'." She piled the counter with as much as it would hold.

Debbie rang in a long skinny bologna, a package of chicken parts, a huge head of cabbage and four loaves of bread.

Mrs. Molloy continued to heap her things on the counter. Her hands seemed a little steadier now. Her last three items were a set of water glasses, two colouring books and a spray can of air freshener. As Debbie was checking them through, Mr. Marshall arrived again. He should get a job at the Arts and Culture, Debbie thought. As a magician. I don't know how good he'd be at making himself vanish but he sure can appear out of nowhere.

He looked at the groceries waiting to be packed, glanced at Debbie and then turned toward Mrs. Molloy. "You must have had quite an order on Saturday," he said. "Didn't you get any of it?"

"I got a few things," she said, not looking at him. "But the majority of it wasn't there. I shoulda noticed it at the time but I was so addled with the youngsters I didn't know if I was comin' or goin'."

"Miss Evans," said Mr. Marshall. He always called the girls Miss when there were customers around. "Miss Evans, did you serve this...lady...on Saturday?"

Mrs. Molloy looked at Debbie and then looked quickly down into the empty cart.

"I had a busy evening, Mr. Marshall. I can hardly remember."

He turned toward Mrs. Molloy. "Who served you? You should remember that."

"I told you, I had that much on my mind...."

"That's a lot of groceries you've got there, madam. And not all groceries, either. I've never noticed you picking up drinking glasses or colouring books before." He leaned over her and said softly, "I asked you to pick up only what you didn't get on Saturday. Are you sure you're being strictly honest about this?"

Debbie realized she was holding her breath as she waited for Mrs. Molloy's answer.

"You never asked that other woman what she picked up on Saturday. I had to buy tumblers Saturday because every onc we had in the house was broke. My daughter was after sendin' me some money and I wanted to get a nice few things in." Her face was still red and shiny but she wasn't shaking at all now.

"Miss Evans. Try to remember, will you, if you served this woman on Saturday. Just take a few minutes to think about it."

Debbie didn't need a few minutes.

"Yes, Mr. Marshall, I did serve her. I remember now."

"Isn't this kind of an unusual order for her?"

"I don't know, sir. It's impossible for me to remember the kind of order everyone in the store gets." She looked him straight in the eye. "She did have more than usual. And I remember those glasses very plain. I thought of buying some for my mother."

"Are you sure, Miss Evans?"

"Of course I'm sure, Mr. Marshall. And if you're not going to believe me, why did you bother to ask?"

Mrs. Molloy, no longer the central figure in the affair, stared at Debbie.

"All right, then. We'll let it go for this time. But we've just got to be more careful about people's groceries going astray." He walked away from the check-out, his back very stiff.

Debbie began to bag the groceries. Mrs. Molloy was still standing beside the conveyor-belt. She glanced at Debbie and said, "Thanks a lot, miss." Then she looked away again.

"That's all right." Debbie felt uncomfortable, no, not uncomfortable, embarrassed. Then, as she wrapped the glasses individually, she caught Mrs. Molloy's eye and they smiled at each other.

"You let her get away with it," said Phyllis that afternoon when they were both waiting in line to punch out.

"What do you mean, I let her get away with it? She only picked up what she didn't get Saturday."

"Is that right, now? You don't say." Although Phyllis' voice was mocking there was another note in it too. Understanding? Appreciation? Or just plain amusement?

Debbie said nothing more. She listened, without really paying attention, to the bits of conversation going on around her.

When she got outside, Phyllis was waiting for her on the sidewalk.

"Want a run home, Deb? Dave'll be here in a minute."

"No thanks, I feel like a walk. I can use the fresh air. Besides, Mom never starts to get supper until *Another World* is over."

"You going anywhere tonight?"

"Well, I got typing seven-thirty. And I was thinkin' about askin' Rob if he wants to go down to the Strand later on. It's no cover tonight and the band is really good."

"Thought you'd be too tired for dancin' tonight. There's Dave now. Hold on to your wool, boy, and stop blowin' that almighty horn."

"Better hurry up, girl. No, I don't feel too bad now. Some days are worse than others."

"Well, I better go, I s'pose, or Dave'll have a fit and a half. See you tomorrow."

"So long, Phyl. Take it easy, now."

Phyllis got into the car and Debbie, her purse swinging, began to walk briskly down the road.

One Saturday

The sun awakened Kathleen very early on Saturday morning. The bedroom windows were far too big, making the house chilly in winter, but it was nice now, in May, to feel the warmth streaming in. For a few moments she felt good, luxuriating in the knowledge that she needn't get up yet. Then she remembered her dream.

Once again she had dreamed of having a small baby. It was a boy this time, a round little brown-eyed boy who looked a lot like David had looked when he was a baby. She recalled the feeling of pure joy the dream had released in her, that sensation she had basked in after the birth of each of her children, especially David, the youngest. It was like lying in a warm pool, with sunlight pouring down the way it was pouring through the windows this morning. Each time she'd experienced it she had wished the feeling would last longer.

In spite of the sun the bed felt a little cold, perhaps because Jim was not there to warm his side of it. He had not wanted to go away without her, or said he hadn't. She would have enjoyed the two days on her own in Toronto while he went to his meetings, and the nights in the hotel. But she hadn't been able to go with him because of Gran.

Gran. She had almost forgotten about her. She hoped Gran wouldn't get up too early this morning, at least until she'd finished her own breakfast. Sometimes, as soon as she sat down at the table, she'd hear Gran's cane pounding. Gran rarely rang the little chrome bell they had put on her night-table. She liked to keep up the pretence that she could look after herself.

Kathleen burrowed down into the blankets again, trying to get back into the dream. Sometimes when she dreamed of having a baby she was glad to wake up, for the dream often ended with something dreadful happening to the child. This time it had been all pleasant. Nothing else mattered except herself and the little brown-eyed boy. But she knew that as soon as she was fully awake she'd have to contend with memory.

When she opened her eyes again she found herself staring at the calendar on the wall opposite the bed. In just six days she would have a birthday. She wished it would just pass like any other day, without anyone noticing it. Who wanted to celebrate a fiftieth birthday? For weeks now it had been at the back of her mind, especially when she woke up in the mornings. *In fifteen years I'll be sixty-five. A "senior citizen." In twenty years I'll be seventy.*

Kathleen wasn't a vain woman, had never worried a great deal about her appearance. It wasn't what she looked like that was bothering her. Slogans that she had never seen or read kept framing themselves in her mind. "There's a funeral in your future" was one of them. Every night when she lay close beside Jim, her hand in his, his body heat warming her, she would think of the nights that must come when she would lie without him, or he without her. So many people she knew had died in their fifties, including her own mother.

Was that Gran, trying to make her way out of the kitchen? Surely not already. Perhaps she was only using the commode beside her bed. Jim had made it the summer before when they had realized that Gran couldn't keep hobbling to the bathroom four or five times a night at the insistence of her old, wasted kidneys. Gran had protested at first, as she protested every symbol of her increasing dependence on others, but in the end she'd probably been glad to give in.

Kathleen sat up. The bed no longer held any comfort for her. She pushed her feet into slippers, pulled on her old red chenille dressing gown and went to the bathroom. Gran's door was wide open; since she'd had the stroke she was afraid to have it closed at night. She was lying on her back in the middle of the bed, her mouth open, snoring slightly. She fell asleep easily, like a small child, but rarely slept through the night.

As soon as Kathleen had settled herself at the kitchen table she heard Gran's cane knocking. Damn. Why couldn't she ring the bell instead of pretending that the cane-thumping was accidental? She decided to ignore it for awhile.

112

The cane was pounding now. Kathleen jumped up from the table, threw her tea into the sink and started toward Gran's room.

The old woman was sitting on the edge of the bed, struggling with her dressing gown. The familiar lump of irritation rose in Kathleen's throat as she went to help. It was the same every day. Only screaming or shouting or crying would dissolve that lump but she rarely screamed or shouted or cried. Unless she was out walking, struggling against the wind in a fierce, noisy winter storm, or in the basement with the radio turned up very loud.

Now that Kathleen was in the room, Gran seemed in no hurry to move. This pattern was the same every day, too. More and more lately Gran reminded Kathleen of a very young child who'd do anything for attention.

Kathleen slid the pail out from under the commode, emptied it into the toilet, ran hot soapy water and disinfectant into it and replaced it in its groove. By this time Gran seemed ready to move. Kathleen bent to take the old woman's arm and together she and Gran made their slow progress to the kitchen.

"Did you hear from Jim yet?" Gran asked.

"No, he's not going to phone. I told you that. He'll be back tomorrow night."

"I suppose he got there all right. Where are the boys?"

"Bob had to work today and David is gone off somewhere in the car."

"When is Alison coming home?"

"Not till next Friday, Gran. I told you that every day this week."

Why do I have to let it show so much? Kathleen asked herself as she eased Gran into her chair at the head of the kitchen table. The old woman smelled strongly of stale urine, as she did most mornings.

"Where's David gone in the car? I'll be worrying about him all day now."

And I suppose I won't be. Kathleen felt her face tighten. Gran must think her flippant and hard, the way she always made a great point of not showing concern when the children were away. The more Gran fretted, the more callous Kathleen forced herself to feel.

She poured Gran's orange juice and tea, gave her some bran flakes and counted out her blood pressure pills. Then she poured more tea for herself, made fresh toast and sat down opposite the old woman.

113

Is she my punishment for what I did six years ago? Gran, of course, knew nothing about that. She thought Kathleen had gone into the hospital for a tubal ligation. She would have been appalled at the idea of abortion. Kathleen remembered the dreadful story about her own abortion Dory Previn had told in one of her books, when the priest with the kindly-sounding Irish name had screamed at Dory that what she'd done at seventeen was the same as taking an infant and bashing its head against a concrete sidewalk. She'd been given a penance and cast out of the confession box.

Kathleen had never in her life tried to get pregnant. It had always amused her to hear about people who had trouble conceiving. When, at forty-four, she found herself pregnant for the fifth time, she couldn't believe it. She had always been very careful, she and Jim had been elaborately careful, but the pregnancy had happened anyway.

They had been camping when it happened, she and Jim. David had been with them but had left the camper to play baseball with some of the boys he'd met in the park. Kathleen almost laughed aloud as she recalled how she had enjoyed that session more than she'd enjoyed sex for months. It sounded so Total Woman, husband and wife alone in the wilderness, she making herself into a vamp for him. It also reminded her of what some of her mother's friends used to say about paying for your pleasure.

She looked now at the old woman eating her cereal, drinking her tea, her eyes wearing that glazed-over expression they had worn so often since the strokes. Gran had experienced more hardship in the twenty years after her young husband was killed than most people did in a lifetime. But she had never known the guilt of deliberately cutting off the life of another human creature.

Gran seemed to have finished her breakfast now. She was sitting back in her chair, her head nodding forward, her tongue protruding through almost-closed lips. Kathleen knew that soon she'd begin to drool. She looked quickly away.

The baby in the dream had looked so much like David. Where was David today? She hadn't been able to resist letting him have the car, with the weather so beautiful. She didn't really know where he had gone, as she so often didn't know, those days, about what David and Bob were doing. On weekends especially she found it hard to get to sleep, and had over and over again imagined the knock on the door, the policeman and the minister waiting when she opened it, just as they had been waiting for Mary Lawton the time her son and his friend had been killed when their car went over the bridge after they left the Ocean View Lounge. When Kathleen finally heard the basement door squeak open, and David's heavy footsteps as he pounded up over the stairs to the bathroom, or Bob's quieter, slower ones, she would whisper, "Thank you, Jesus," too full of relief to even laugh at herself for saying it.

Gran was ready to go back to the bedroom now.

"What's it like out?" she asked as they walked through the hall. She asked that every morning.

"Nice and sunny," said Kathleen, her throat hurting again. "A bit cool, though."

"We won't get out today, I don't s'pose. Not with the car gone," Gran sighed heavily. "It's going to be a long day for me."

And what kind of a day do you think it's going to be for me, you smelly old thing? Kathleen was always glad nobody could hear what was in her mind. Do you think I exactly enjoy staying here looking after you, too much to do, not enough to do, worrying about David and trying not to let you know it, grieving over things you know nothing about? Do you think it's going to be the highlight of my life or something? She turned away so that Gran wouldn't see the anger in her face.

She thought of a television program she'd seen a few nights earlier, the one about that near-saint Mother Teresa, who was spending her life looking after the sick and the dying. It must be done with love, she had insisted, this frail, sexless creature in her long, loose robe. Didn't Mother Teresa ever get angry, frustrated, annoyed in spite of herself with the poor pathetic creatures who were dying all around her? It's probably easier to help people to die than to help them to live, Kathleen had thought as she watched the program. And then had felt immediately ashamed of herself.

Lately she'd been reading a lot of magazine articles that advised her, and other women like her, not to be too hard on themselves. She remembered one piece titled "The One Person You Can't Forgive." Well, the Right-to-Lifers didn't make things any easier, that was certain. Almost every time she opened a newspaper these days she'd see a letter headed "Baby Murders Must Stop!" or "Gas Chambers Next" or "Abortion Today, Euthanasia Tomorrow!" That last one almost made her laugh, when she could stop being angry or keep from crying. Here she was, tied day after day to the needs of an old woman who could no longer look after herself. And she'd been doing this for five years.

She thought again about Dory Previn and wondered if she herself had agreed to look after Gran as a kind of penance for her own "sin." She had never been a Roman Catholic but the stern Protestantism that was her background could be even harder to live with at times, the way it left everything up to your conscience.

Gran's bell rang, sounding louder than usual. Kathleen swore to herself and tried hard to arrange her features in a pleasant expression before she went into the bedroom. At least she'd abandoned the cane-knocking strategy.

"Where's Bob today?" Gran was sitting up again now. She never stayed lying down for long.

"I told you, Gran, he's working. All day."

"Poor boy, he's going to wear himself out, working and going to university too. It's too much."

"He needs the money." Kathleen wondered what would have to happen to her before the old woman saw *her* as tired, weary exhausted? To Gran, Kathleen was a provider for Jim, David, Alison, Bob, herself, the cat, and Margot by a kind of remote control. What could she do if I collapsed on the floor in front of her eyes?

"Did you hear from Margot this week?"

"I had a letter yesterday, Gran. Don't you remember? I showed it to you."

"If you did I couldn't read it. My eyes are shockin' here lately."

Kathleen picked up a crumpled tissue from the floor and threw it into the wastebasket. She found balled-up tissues like that every morning, sometimes several. Did Gran cry in the night?

She helped the old woman to get dressed. Afterwards Gran, exhausted from even that much effort, lay back on her pillows.

Back in the living room, Kathleen sat down in the armchair and closed her eyes. She thought of the hours she'd spent sitting in that same chair during those horrible weeks after she'd had the abortion and tubal ligation. Every day she'd put in the morning talking to her sister Audrey and her friends Jean and Daphne on the telephone. Not Angela, though. Angela was a practising Catholic. Those conversations had helped her to get through the hours until David came home to lunch.

Gran's bell rang again. She was sitting on the bed, her eyes staring straight ahead at something that wasn't there. Her eyes, and the set of her shoulders, reminded Kathleen of a sheep that she and Jim had come upon once when they were walking over the hills in Brigus. Or maybe it had been a lamb. Gran was obviously waiting to be led out to the living room. Why couldn't she stay in one place?

On the radio in the living room, the announcer was reading a short item about the ever-increasing price of gold.

"Can you buy five-dollar gold pieces now?" Gran asked. "I had a five-dollar gold piece once," she went on, not waiting for a reply. "Poor Eldred gave it to me. I treasured it for years but then one time when I was having it hard I had to spend it on groceries." The old woman's eyes filled with tears; they didn't look like a sheep's eyes, or a lamb's, any longer. She reached into her cardigan pocket for her glasses. Her brother Eldred had died in the First World War.

Kathleen didn't know if she wanted to cry herself, or scream. She was used to most of Gran's stories, but this was a new one. She turned and went into the kitchen to make lunch.

The rest of the day passed slowly. After lunch she settled Gran down in the big armchair, her puffy feet on the carpet-covered footstool Jim had made for her. Kathleen herself lay down on the chesterfield. She was always tired these days; Dr. O'Malley thought she might have a thyroid deficiency. She let her eyelids drop as she listened to the regular Saturday afternoon music program on the radio.

The sun was still streaming in through the picture window. Basking in the sun this way, basking almost as a cat basks, she could forget for the moment that it wasn't really very warm out, that it was just a trick of sunlight through the glass. She felt herself relaxing as she almost dozed, listening to the Nashville performers sing of poverty and desertion and lost love. From her almost-sleep, she glanced across at Gran. The old woman's eyes were closed, her mouth slightly open. She seemed at peace, for the moment.

Loretta Lynn's true country voice came over the airwaves, tuneful and clear:

> They say to have her hair done Liz flies all the way to France.
> And Jackie's seen in a discothèque, doing a brand new dance,
> And the White House social season should be busy and gay,
> But here in Topeka, the rain is a-fallin',
> The faucet is a drippin' and the kids are a-bawlin',
> One of 'em's a-toddlin' and one is a-crawlin'
> And one's on the way.

A cloud passed over the sun; Kathleen brushed hot tears from her eyes. Nowadays she often got weepy, especially when she passed the school where the children had gone, wishing back the days when they'd all been dependent on her. When she'd actually been living through those days she couldn't wait for them to end.

Strange, wasn't it, to have such mixed feelings about one's children? After they were born it was difficult to remember a time when they hadn't been around. To realize that they might never have been born, that chance plays so crucial a part in the making of a human being, was almost impossible. Yet, when her pregnancy had been confirmed six years before, when she'd realized it was possible for her to have a therapeutic abortion, she had known immediately that she would not have this baby.

Now Dolly Parton was singing *Coat of Many Colours*. That woeful, strangely poignant story about a child's shattered pride in a new homemade coat brought her attention back to Gran. Jim often joked now that he and his brother Albert had once shared a coat. The old woman was hunched forward in the chair now, her eyes open, staring at the window.

"Do you want anything, Gran?" she forced herself to say.

"No, nothing I can have. I wouldn't mind a new pair of legs." Sometimes Gran chuckled when she said things like that, but not today. "What wouldn't I give to be able to go out. People with nothing wrong with them don't appreciate what a blessing it is to be able to go and come when they want to." For once Kathleen had sense enough to say nothing.

Sometimes she felt herself rushing headlong into old age, following the path that Gran had worn for her. How long would it be before someone had to lead her from room to room, help her to get dressed, empty her slops? Of course Alison or Margot or Bob or David wouldn't ever have to do for her what she had to do for Gran. She'd rather die, or go into the most impersonal institution in the country. She would make her own decisions, not force others to make them for her. Or so she believed now.

The music was soft and seductive; Kathleen felt herself being lulled into sleep. The room, with the sun still pouring in, looked strange and foreign the way an operating room and the people in it look as the patient is being sucked under by the anaesthetic.

When she woke up, the sun was gone. It wouldn't be dark for hours yet; Daylight Saving Time had started a week before. But there was something about the suddenly heavy sky, the dark clouds, the absence of sun, that reminded Kathleen of an evening in winter. Perhaps it was going to rain, or even snow. She hoped it wouldn't snow before David got back with the car. She had told Jim it was too early to take off the snow tires. They often had snow in May.

The menace that had been hovering over her all day came closer as she started to get supper. Perhaps it was the sudden blackness of the sky, or her preoccupation with David and the car. Would he and his friend Mike stop for a few beers? Were they even now rolling joints for themselves? The cigarette papers that she had noticed in David's room a few days before were not there today.

Kathleen fixed her eyes on Gran, sitting across from her at the kitchen table, eating with appetite the cod chowder Kathleen had put in front of her. Food was one of the few things left for the old woman to enjoy.

Bob phoned to say he'd be staying the night at a friend's apartment. He often stayed downtown on weekends. Kathleen had almost given up speculating about where he was, or what he was doing, reminding herself that most young men of twenty-one did not even live at home. Gran often asked Bob why he didn't get a nice girlfriend for himself; even though the question always angered Kathleen, she couldn't help wondering the same thing herself.

She was really beginning to worry about David now. Just as she had expected, it had started to snow; the flakes were getting thicker. He'd had his driver's license for less than a year.

What's it all about? she asked herself, staring through the window at the snow. We're born, we grow up, we have children, we worry about them, they grow up, we worry about our parents, they die, we grow old, our children worry about us, we die. How senseless it all is.

"Isn't David home yet?" Gran called from her chair in the darkening living room. She hadn't wanted the light on, claiming it hurt her eyes.

Kathleen considered telling her a lie but instead decided to be flip. "So that's your worry for today, is it, Gran?" she said lightly. She thought of the little wooden plaque she'd bought for Gran on her last hurried trip out of town. "Don't just sit there, worry," it said in large, fancy letters, cut deep into the wood.

119

"It must be wonderful not to worry," Gran said, tightening her mouth.

Yes, thought Kathleen, it must be.

As she and the old woman sat watching television, Kathleen tried hard to concentrate on the *Barney Miller* rerun that even Gran was laughing at but she couldn't keep her mind off the slippery, winding road that David must be driving over. If something happens, it happens. Worrying won't prevent it. All the clichés she used on Gran and other people crowded into her head but, like most of the clichés used in times of stress and sorrow, they did her absolutely no good.

When she had finally made up her mind to call Mrs. Burton, mother of David's friend Mike, she heard the familiar squeak of the basement door. David ran up the stairs and bounded into the living room.

"What have you got it so dark for?" he asked, switching on the light.

"Where *were* you, David?" his grandmother asked. "I was worried about you."

"Yes, you know what Gran is like." Kathleen was surprised at the ease of her laughter.

"What's for supper, Mom?" David went into the kitchen. "Hi, cat, what're you at?" He picked up the cat who had followed him upstairs, ruffling the thick black fur.

"There's some chowder on the stove," Kathleen said. "But perhaps you'd rather have bacon and eggs. I didn't know what time you were coming." She kept her voice light. "You didn't tell us where you were."

"Oh, here and there. And I'd love some bacon and eggs, if it's okay with you. Sunny side up now, remember." He grinned at her, his brown eyes shining, and Kathleen thought of the baby in her dream.

"You've got great times," she said to David, putting the iron frying pan on the burner, and remembering her mother saying the same thing to her.

Mike came over, and he and David spent the evening in the basement recreation room. The sound of rock music and laughter thundered up through the hot air vents. Jim phoned, although he'd said he wasn't going to. Even more surprising, Margot, who rarely called home, phoned also, sounding a little bit lonely. Then, just before Gran went to her room for the night, her only daughter, Jim's sister Iris, called from Montreal where she'd been living for five years.

"Good night, now," Gran said finally into the phone, her voice sounding stronger than it had all day. "We're doing well with the phone calls tonight," she said to Kathleen. Just for a moment there was the kind of cameraderie that existed so rarely between the two women.

"Good night, now," Gran repeated later as Kathleen tucked her into bed. She seemed about to say something more but changed her mind.

"Good night, Gran," Kathleen felt inclined to kiss the old woman. Instead she smoothed her hair and adjusted the two pillows under her head. "I hope you sleep well."

"So do I," said Gran, turning on her side.

In the living room the drapes were drawn, shutting out the dark and the snow. From the basement Pink Floyd sang out a musical sermon to the materialistic world. The boys were laughing a lot; Kathleen had heard that smoking pot made people laugh at nothing. She wouldn't worry about that tonight.

She got some orange juice and chocolate biscuits from the kitchen, and settled down to watch televison. Another night that there'd be no clergyman and policeman at the door to bring her bad news. As for the bad news locked up inside her, that was contained, for the time being. "Thank you, Jesus," she whispered, giggling to herself. And, for once taking no thought for tomorrow, she leaned back against the cushions, an unlikely lily of the field.